VIRTUALLY
CHRISTMAS

Books by David Baddiel

ANIMALCOLM

BIRTHDAY BOY

(THE BOY WHO GOT) ACCIDENTALLY FAMOUS

FUTURE FRIEND

HEAD KID

THE PARENT AGENCY

THE PERSON CONTROLLER

THE TAYLOR TURBOCHASER

VIRTUALLY CHRISTMAS

ONLY CHILDREN

VIRTUALLY CHRISTMAS

DAVID BADDIEL

Illustrated by Steven Lenton

HarperCollins *Children's Books*

First published in the United Kingdom by
HarperCollins *Children's Books* in 2022
Published in this edition in 2023
HarperCollins *Children's Books* is a division of HarperCollins*Publishers* Ltd
1 London Bridge Street
London SE1 9GF

www.harpercollins.co.uk

HarperCollins*Publishers*
Macken House, 39/40 Mayor Street Upper
Dublin 1, D01 C9W8, Ireland

1

ISBN 978-0-00-833432-1

Typeset in ITC Novarese Book 12/22pt
Printed and bound in the UK using 100% renewable electricity
at CPI Group (UK) Ltd
A CIP catalogue record for this title is available from the British Library.

To my son Ezra, for the idea. Again. At some point, I'm going to have to pay him.

CHAPTER 1

Santa! Santa!

It should've been amazing, Santa himself appearing in Etta Baxter's living room.

'Ho ho ho!' he said, in his booming Santa voice. 'How are you, Etta?'

That *was* amazing, right? Santa knowing her name? But for some reason, Etta – an eleven-year-old girl with glasses and dark hair, who was currently staring at Santa with fairly bored eyes – didn't seem that amazed. Her little brother Jonas, who was three and a half: *he* was. He'd been shouting: 'Santa! Santa! Santa! Santa!' non-stop since Santa appeared.

'Have you been a good girl this year?' Santa continued. 'Your mum says you have. And I *know* you've been a great owner for Weech!'

Weech was Etta's kitten, so called because of the tiny high-pitched noise he made that wasn't quite a meow. That too – Santa knowing something so detailed about Etta's life – should've been amazing. But Etta's eyes didn't brighten. And Etta's eyes were normally very bright indeed.

'Santa! Santa! Santa!' said Jonas.

'Ho ho ho, Jonas,' said Santa. 'I'll come to you in a minute. But meanwhile . . . Etta. I know exactly what you want for Christmas this year. A new sparkly collar for Weech! One with green and red jewels all round it!'

'You do want that, don't you, E?' said Etta's mum, whose name was Bonny. Bonny was crouching down next to Etta. She was pulling that face that grown-ups make when they want you to be pleased about something, but are not sure if you in fact are. You know the face.

Etta nodded. But it wasn't a very enthusiastic nod.

'And I will make sure you get it!' said Santa.

'Wow, Santa!' said her mum. 'Thank you!'

'Santa! Santa!' This wasn't Etta. It was Jonas. You probably knew that by now.

'No problem for me or my elves!' said Santa.

Etta continued just to stare coldly at Santa. This was getting a bit awkward.

'Etta . . . isn't it amazing that Santa has come to see us and that he knows exactly what you want for Christmas?' said Bonny, her voice becoming a bit pleading. 'Don't you want to thank him . . . at least?'

'OK,' said Etta, speaking at last. Her voice was deadpan. 'I'll tell you what . . .' she carried on, much in the same tone, 'I'll give Santa a hug.'

'Um . . .' said her mum.

'Santa! Santa!'

'Come on, Santa,' said Etta, opening her arms.

'I'm not sure that's . . . allowed . . .?' said Bonny.

'Ho ho ho!' said Santa, but without moving towards her.

'What are you laughing at?' said Etta. 'I'm not suggesting a *funny* hug.'

'Well . . .' said Santa. 'It's kind of my catchphrase. *Ho ho ho.* I say it all the time.'

'But it is still you laughing, right?'

'Um . . . yes . . . I guess.'

'So why do it at something that isn't funny?'

Santa frowned. He turned to Bonny for help. She shrugged. He looked to Jonas.

'Santa!' shouted Jonas.

'Ho ho . . . ho?'

'Right,' said Etta. 'Anyway. About that hug . . .' She

opened her arms again and moved towards Santa. Santa looked worried. Etta reached where he was standing, by the fireplace. She put her arms round him, and then . . . put her arms through him. Like he was a ghost. Like he wasn't, in fact, there.

'OK,' said Santa. 'Good hug. Lovely. Anyway, gotta rush. No rest for the . . . non-wicked!'

And he vanished. Disappeared.

'Santa?' said Jonas.

Etta's mum looked at Etta.

'E!' she said. 'You've scared Santa off!'

'Well,' said Etta, 'it's not my fault he's a hologram.'

At which point Jonas burst into tears.

CHAPTER 2
Winterzone

'Hi. Gary?' said Bryan Leaf.

'Er . . . yes, sir. Gary Baxter.'

'No need to tell me your surname,' said Bryan. 'We go by first names here at Winterzone.'

'OK, sir.'

'And obviously, chuck that *sir* thing. Call me Bryan. Bry, in fact, is what I prefer. As I'm sure you know.'

Gary did know. He had worked for Winterzone

for ten years. And every time Bryan Leaf came onstage at the Winterzone Global Conference, beamed every first of November to one hundred countries simultaneously, across every social media platform, a massive screen always came up behind him with the word 'Bry' on it. Plus he left the stage to the tune of a song by Winterzone's in-house band called 'I'm Dreaming of a Bry-te Christmas.'

'OK . . . Bry.' It still sounded weird, though, no matter how many times Gary heard it.

Bry had his usual expression on his face: smiley, and kind, but with a sense that he had looked in the mirror for a long time and worked out what a smiley and kind expression was. He was completely bald, and so it looked like someone had painted a – very studied – smiley kind expression on a big egg.

Next to Bry stood his personal assistant, Raisa. She looked like she always did: like she was thinking of absolutely nothing. Gary knew, however, that this wasn't true. She was thinking of absolutely nothing *except* how to serve Bry and Winterzone. She was dressed, as ever, in an all-white uniform, but also, as ever, had with her a small bright orange handbag strapped across her shoulder. One of her hands always seemed to be resting lightly but firmly on the clasps of this bag, which were a shiny green colour. The clasps, that is, not her hands.

They were standing in the Snowy Space, an enormous room in the centre of the Winterzone building. The Winterzone building stood on its own in many acres of land on the edge of a large city. It was over fifty storeys high and built in the shape of an enormous Christmas tree: an enormous concrete Christmas tree. It had lots of windows, but pride of place went to a very long one that circled the entire front of the top floor of the building. It was made of coloured glass, red and green and white,

and drawn into it was the word WINTERZONE™, surrounded by snowflakes and Santavatars (the name of the holographic Santa that was appearing in Etta's flat) and sleighs. You could see this from almost any point in the city.

Also in the Snowy Space were the other members of Bry's personal team. There was Hamnet, a man who only wore black, and who always brought into work his all-white cockatoo – also called Hamnet – who was currently sitting on his shoulder. Then there was Fester, a woman who seemed to Gary to be about fourteen, but was actually in her late fifties – her teenage appearance being entirely due to her diet of super-vitamin shakes, one of which she was just finishing (it was very bright green and had the words **VEGGY HEALTHY** on the bottle). And finally there was CWX25. CWX25 was a robot, but looked like a human, who was programmed to think mainly about Christmas. The robot wore a red and green sweater with reindeer and snowflakes on it.

'Sit, Gary. Sit!' said Bry.

Gary looked around.

'On the beanbag. Obvs.'

'Ob——?' began Gary.

'It's short for "obviously",' said Bry. 'Obvs.'

'Right, right,' said Gary.

He sat down. The beanbag was an enormous red oblong in the middle of the room. It had white fur round the edges of it. No one else in the Snowy Space was sitting, so it felt very strange for him to do so. Gary sank into the beanbag. It was absurdly deep. He wondered if he would ever be able to get out of it. Also, he was wearing a suit, which, sitting on a beanbag, felt wrong. Then again, he always felt wrong wearing a suit at Winterzone. Most other people wore loose clothing, T-shirts and baggy pants, although company policy preferred these to be in red, green and white – Christmassy – combinations.

Bry, as ever, was barefoot.

'Comfy, right?' said Bry.

'Um . . .'

'So, Gary, I guess you're wondering why I called you here?'

'Well . . . I thought it might be something to do with the new Super-Sleigh we've been designing at TinselTech 1. It's amazing – it can travel at twenty times the speed of sound . . .'

Raisa stared at him. Gary could make out, even from his position too far into the beanbag, a small shake of her head.

'No, Gary,' said Bry. 'It's not that. As you know, ever since we at Winterzone took over Christmas . . . since we, you know, decided to, you know, *modernise* the whole festival, we've strived to make this, the most wonderful time of the year . . .'

'TM, Winterzone,' said Raisa.

'Sorry?' said Gary.

'We've trademarked it,' she said, in her accent that Gary could never entirely place, but which sounded like, in another universe, would definitely belong to a spy. '*The most wonderful time of the year. We own that saying now.*'

'Right,' said Bry. 'Well, that's my point, Gary – it IS the most wonderful time of the year . . .'

'Oh, so true,' said Hamnet. 'Right, Hamnet?'

'Most wonderful time of the year!' screeched Hamnet. The cockatoo.

'So correct!' said Fester, although it was quite hard to hear, as she was glugging a new super-vitamin shake. This one had the words **BERRY GOOD FOR YOU** written on it.

'It's the most . . . wonderful time of the year!' sang CWX25. 'The most wonderful time of the year! THE MOST WONDERFUL TIME—'

'Can someone switch him off?' whispered Bry. Raisa, without changing her expression, took out a tiny remote control and pressed a button.

'OF THE YE—' sang CWX25, and then stopped, his mouth frozen open. Everyone went quiet. Gary looked at the robot. He – the robot – looked like someone who had yawned and then got stuck, permanently, in mid-yawn.

'Sorry, Bry,' said Hamnet. The human. 'CWX25 has got a bit of a glitch with songs. Soon as he hears them, something in the circuitry makes him want to sing them over and over again. Like an ear worm.'

'Is there a worm? In his ear? Can I have it?' said Hamnet. The cockatoo. You could probably guess that.

'Um . . . I could take a look at CWX25, if you like,' said Gary. 'In TinselTech 1.'

'I think not!' said Hamnet.

'Think not!' screeched Hamnet.

'We can take care of him in TinselTech 2!' said Hamnet.

'TINSELTECH 2!' screeched Hamnet.

'Oh, you run TinselTech 2?' said Gary, who had never known that before. Or indeed that they were responsible for making the robot.

'Well, I do,' said Hamnet. 'The cockatoo doesn't.'

'I don't?!' screeched Hamnet.

'Anyway,' said Gary, looking back to Bry, 'of course. I agree. About the wonderful time of the year thing. So that's why we in TinselTech 1 think the Super-Sleigh will be an amazing—'

'Can you shut up about that, Gary?' said Bry, still with his smiley, kindly face on, even though he was, clearly, not saying something smiley and kind. 'I mean, no one's actually going to be *using* it,' he continued. 'Because we have an army of delivery drones. The sleigh's just a branding thing. For memes, and ads. You know that, right?'

Gary nodded. Although he looked like he hadn't quite known that, until this moment. He had assumed that someone – perhaps even Bry? – would ride it. That it would be used to deliver presents across the sky somehow.

'Here's the thing. That is the thing.' Bry said the word 'thing' a lot. 'Thing is: you have a daughter, right?'

'Um . . . yes?' said Gary.

Bry nodded. Raisa handed him a bottle of water. It said **WW**. Which stood for **WINTERZONE WATER**. He took a tiny sip of it.

'This one?' said Bry.

Raisa took the tiny remote stick out again. A large screen appeared out of nowhere, hovering behind Bry. Gary looked at it. On the screen was . . . Etta. And Bonny, crouching next to her.

'OK,' said Etta, on the screen. 'I'll give Santa a hug.'

'Um . . .' said Bonny, next to her.

'Santa! Santa!'

Raisa paused the picture.

'Who's that speaking?' said Raisa to Gary.

'Uh . . . it's my son, Jonas. He's not in the frame. Of the shot.'

'I see. The name Santa is of course trademarked to Winterzone too. Is he aware of that?'

'Um . . . he's three and a half?'

Raisa stared at him. Her expression, without changing, somehow managed to say: *So?* She clicked on her remote.

'Come on, Santa,' Etta said onscreen, opening her arms.

'I'm not sure that's . . . allowed . . . ?' said Bonny.

'Ho ho ho!' said a voice. As it spoke, Gary could see white-gloved hands, and a white fur trim on the edge of some red sleeves, rise up towards Etta from behind the camera.

Raisa paused the picture again. Everyone looked at Gary. They all seemed to be frowning in displeasure. Even CWX25, although that may just have been what his face looked like when he was switched off.

'Thing is, you'll know . . .' said Bry, ' . . . that the Santavatars—'

'Also trademarked,' said Raisa.

'—are able to record content from any house they visit.'

'Yes,' said Gary. 'We developed that capability in TinselTech 1 as well, and—'

Bry waved him away. 'Whatevs. No one is responsible for any one idea here, Gary.'

'Everyone's idea is everyone's idea,' said Raisa, as if this was a company slogan. Which it was, except at Winterzone slogans were called *mantras*.

'EVERYONE'S IDEA IS EVERYONE'S IDEA!' screeched Hamnet. The cockatoo.

'Exactly,' said Bry. 'Well, everyone's idea is kind of *my* idea. As I own the company. But it's the same thing.'

'IT'S THE SAME THING!' screeched Hamnet.

'Shh, Hamnet,' said Hamnet.

'I don't want to play you the whole film,' Bry continued, 'but basically, your daughter – Etta, right?'

'Yes,' said Gary.

'Etta – middle name Elsa – aged eleven years, two months, thirteen days,' said Raisa. 'I have her online profile here . . .'

'Yep,' said Bry, waving Raisa away, 'her. She got very . . . weird about being visited by that Santavatar. She—'

'Yes,' sighed Gary. 'I know what she will have been like.'

There was a pause. Following a tiny nod from Bry, Raisa clicked the remote, and the screen vanished. Bry smiled.

'Well, as you know, Gary, working for Winterzone isn't just about *working* for Winterzone. Work – play – life – at Winterzone, especially at the most wonderful time of the year, is all one. And family. Wow. Family. Eh, Raisa?'

Raisa blinked.

'Family really matters' she said expressionlessly. It was another company mantra.

'Oh, yeah,' said Hamnet. 'Family really matters.'

'FAMILY REALLY—'

'Shh, Hamnet.'

'Family. Really. Matters.' This was CWX25, who had somehow self-activated. His voice was slowing down though and was much lower in pitch than it should be.

'You're *sure* you don't want me to have a look at CWX . . .' said Gary, but stopped after a sharp stare from Hamnet. The cockatoo. Hamnet the human was pretending not to have heard.

'Family really matters,' said Fester, opening a new super-vitamin bottle – **MINTY MENTAL MAGIC** – with her very young-looking hands. 'I was just saying that to my grandchildren.'

'Your grandchildren . . .?' began Gary, but then thought better of saying any more. 'But yes, I agree: family does really matter.'

Bry smiled again.

'Exactly. And the best way to ensure your family is having the most wonderful time they could possibly have at the most wonderful time of the year is to insist that they totally buy into Winterzone's version of the most wonderful time of the year. That they fully and completely embrace Winterzone wonderfulness.' Here, his smile faded suddenly. 'That they don't, in other words, shut down Winterzone's wonderfulness with some cynical, frankly disruptive, behaviour that makes one of our Santavatars look . . . not real.'

'Right, right,' said Gary. 'But it's not like anyone's going to see her doing that?'

Bry frowned. 'I saw it, Gary. I saw it.' He gestured to his right. 'And now Raisa, and Fester, and Hamnet, and Hamnet, and CWX25 have seen it.'

'OK, but one of them is a cockatoo,' said Gary. 'And another one a robot.'

'Anyone could have seen it,' said Raisa, interjecting. 'We put all the Santavatar footage online.' She looked with sudden hardness at Gary. 'Because most of the children's reactions are so *delightful*.'

'Hmm,' said Bry. 'Most of them, Gary. Most of

them.' He took a deep breath. 'But we'd like that to be *all* of them. We particularly would like that to be all of the children who are the children of people who work at Winterzone. Because children of Winterzone employees dissing Winterzone's Christmas is not a good look. Remember, Gary: Christmas begins at home.'

Gary frowned. 'I think that's . . . charity?'

Bry gave a tiny shake of the head. 'It's Christmas. Everything's about Christmas.'

Raisa turned to Bry and whispered something.

'Hey!' said Bry. 'Great thought. We could underline how much Etta's attitude has changed by making her the Perfect Present Please kid this year. OK, Gary?'

Gary frowned again, worried. Perfect Present Please was a tradition at Winterzone. Every Christmas Eve, one child was chosen to come to Winterzone headquarters, and, on a large stage and beamed around the world, got to ask for their perfect present. They did this by saying the words: 'I'd like my perfect present, please, which is . . .' And then, by the magic of Winterzone technology, that present would be delivered to them, wrapped and ready, before they even left the stage.

Most children would kill – well, maybe not *kill*, but certainly fight at quite a dangerous level – to be the Perfect Present Please kid. However, as Gary knew, which is why he was frowning, Etta was not most children. Certainly not in regard to Christmas, or at least Christmas as it was these days.

'OK, Gary?' said Bry again. His smile was fixed.

'Yes . . . well, thing is, Etta is quite a headstrong girl – and my relationship with her is . . . well, I actually split from my wife a few years back and—'

'OK, Gary?' Bry repeated, with a strong sense of *This is the last time I'm saying this*. He never stopped smiling, but his eyes and his voice became very hard indeed.

Gary gulped.

'OK, Bryan,' he said.

'Bry,' said Bry, walking away.

Gary looked around. All the others were also walking away, apart from Raisa, who looked on at him impassively. A minute – and a fair amount of shifting about – later, Gary said:

'Raisa . . . can you help me out of the beanbag?'

'No,' said Raisa, now also walking away.

CHAPTER 3

A bit difficult

It was always a bit difficult, Etta found, when her dad came round to their flat. It was awkward between him and Etta's mum since they had split up, and also she knew it meant that her dad wanted to have a big talk with her about something. No kid loves it when their parents want to do a big talk, and Etta was no different. In fact, if anything, she was a bit worse than most kids in the big-talk situation, as most kids are pretty good at nodding their heads and saying 'Yes, Dad' or 'Yes, Mum' until it's over. But Etta was not.

'Look, Etta, I don't understand what your problem is,' her dad was saying. He was pacing around the living room. 'Every other kid *loves* the Santavatars.'

'Do they? How do you know?'

'Because we . . .'

'By "we", do you mean Winterzone?'

'Yes . . . we . . . the company I work for . . . have done a lot of market research, and we've discovered that the Santavatars hold a ninety-five per cent approval rating for over seventy per cent of under-elevens.'

'Oh, Gary,' said Bonny.

'What?' asked Gary.

'Do you really have to speak like that?'

'Like what?'

'In statistics.'

'Oh. I suppose you're going to say that's why you divorced me?'

'No, but it didn't help.'

'Well, thank you very much.'

'Compared to what?' said Etta.

'Pardon?' said Bonny.

'Pardon?' said Gary.

'Those statistics about how much kids love the computerised – the hologram Santas . . .' said Etta.

'The Santavatars, yes?'

'Did you ask them how much they loved them compared to the *real* Santa?'

Etta's mum and dad looked at each other uncomfortably.

'The real Santa?' said Bonny eventually.

'Yes!' said Etta. 'You know. The one that did all the presents and was the . . . the big daddy of Christmas before Winterzone took over everything. The one who lived in Lapland with elves and reindeer!'

Gary frowned. 'How do you even *know* about him?' he said. 'Winterzone has run Christmas since before you were born . . .'

Etta stared at him. 'Dad. You say you work for Winterzone. Who have basically taken the entire heart and soul out of Christmas and put it online, for money.'

'Etta, that's unfair—'

'But despite that, you seem not to have heard of something called *the internet*?' said Etta.

'Oh. OK.'

'I'm surprised Winterzone haven't shut it down,' Etta continued. 'But while they haven't, hey, Dad – the *real* Santa has still got an Infopedia page. On which it says, by the way, that no one knows where he is any more. But that doesn't mean Santa's dead!'

'Santa's dead! Santa's dead!' came a cry. 'Waaaaaaaahhh!'

'Oh no, Etta,' said Bonny. 'You've woken up Jonas. He was having a nap.'

CHAPTER 4

Do not open until Christmas

There was a silence between Etta and her father after her mum left the room. He looked at her moodily.

'What happened, Etta? You used to love Christmas...'

Etta shook her head. 'Dad – I still love Christmas. Just not *Winterzone's* Christmas.'

'But Winterzone's Christmas is great!' said Gary. 'Hey, I remember Christmas like it used to be. It was so much *work*. Buying presents from shops . . .

wrapping them up . . . humping a real tree into the house . . . queuing for ages at grottos to see fat middle-aged men dressed up as Santa . . . We had to eat something called turkey that was always, always dry . . . We had these things called crackers that we had to pull, with the worst paper hats and the worst jokes *ever* written inside them . . .'

Christmas, it was true, wasn't like this any more. Now, most families spent the weeks leading up to Christmas in front of all their different screens, using the various sites and apps provided by Winterzone. There was an app, PresentR, on which children could tap in their Christmas list, and this automatically linked up with Xmasmart, the shopping site where all the presents mentioned could be instantly found and bought. They would all be delivered by Zonedrones, on Christmas Eve, in special Winterzone cardboard packaging in the shape of a stocking. The Zonedrones were coloured red and white and played

little electronic versions of Christmas songs as they flew about the place. Sometimes Etta would look up and see lots of them hovering around houses, banging into each other to the tune of 'I Believe in Father Christmas'. On Christmas Day itself, everyone would have all their screens on, and relatives would join the festivities electronically.

Winterzone also broadcast a continuous Snowing Channel, so you could, if you wanted, put a screen up on the wall, like a window, and make it seem like it was a proper white Christmas outside, even though it never really was, ever since the weather became too hot, even in December. And there were the Santavatars – computerised 3-D Santas, that you could book and have beamed into your house whenever you wanted. Parents could type in lots of information about their child so that, when a Santavatar turned up in their house, it would seem to know lots about them. They were very popular. With most children.

'Yes,' said Etta. 'I know about crackers.' She sighed. 'I didn't really want to show you this. It's probably a bit embarrassing. But . . .' She gestured to her dad to come into her bedroom. He frowned but followed her. Once inside, Etta went over to her bed and crawled under it. She re-emerged seconds later, holding an old white shoebox. On it she had written in purple felt tip, 'Do Not Open Until Christmas', although, as she brought it over to her dad, he could see that she'd inserted another two words. Squashed in with a little arrow between 'Until' and 'Christmas' it said: 'The Real'.

'What's that?' said Gary.

Etta looked at him as if she was still uncertain about whether to show him what was inside. Then she shrugged her shoulders and handed the box to her dad. He took the lid off and looked down. Inside, there was:

A small piece of silver tinsel.

A shiny red bauble, with a little hook on it for hanging on a tree.

A gold Christmas cracker.

And a little crayon drawing of Santa Claus, flying his sleigh across the moon.

CHAPTER 5

Ding-dong
merrily
on high

'I see you've been allowed to view the sacred Christmas box, then . . .' said Bonny, coming back into the room. She was holding Jonas on her shoulder, who had clearly been crying for a while.

'Yes . . .' said Gary. 'Er . . . thank you, Etta.'

Etta shrugged again. Gary put his hand in to take the cracker out.

'Careful!' said Etta. 'It's old . . .'

Gary saw that the cracker was fraying at the edges. He nodded.

'Where did you *get* all this stuff?'

'Grandma Jo gave it to me.'

Gary looked up.

'My mum?'

'Yes.'

Grandma Jo, Gary's mum, had died a couple of years ago. Etta had loved her very much. She had had hair that was a strange blue colour, and glasses that she used to clean with a tiny tissue that she kept up her sleeve. She was small, although she would always say that she had shrunk since she was younger, which always made Etta laugh. Some of Etta's happiest memories as a toddler were of sitting on her grandma's knee and listening to her stories.

'The last Christmas she spent with us . . .'

'Three years ago.'

'Yes . . . she took me aside and gave me all these things. She'd kept them from when she was a little girl. She used to tell me all about Christmas – how it used to be.'

Gary looked down into the box again. He reached in and took out the shiny red bauble. He held it up. You could see both their faces in it.

'She didn't have this from when she was a little girl,' he said quietly.

'She didn't?' asked Etta.

'No. I made it for her . . . when I was a kid.'

He handed it back to Etta. She looked at it with some wonder.

'That's amazing, Dad. How did you do that?'

He smiled. 'I've always been good with my hands, Etta. Always liked to make things.' He looked back down at the box. 'But . . . why did she give them to you?'

Etta fell silent. 'Maybe she knew . . .' said Bonny, coming over. 'That it was going to be her last Christmas.'

Gary nodded. He looked very sad.

'And she could see how much Etta loved Christmas,' continued Bonny. 'So . . .'

'Why didn't she give them to *me*, though?' said Gary.

'Well,' said Etta, 'you've just told me how much you enjoyed Christmas before Winterzone took over. Which was not very much. How much *work* it was.'

Gary opened his mouth to speak.

'And also, you work for *Winterzone*. So . . .' She reached out her arms and took the box back. Etta was always fairly definite about what she did and didn't want – and did and didn't like. She was not a wishy-washy person. Her dad looked at her and wondered if, although this was in some ways a good way to be, he would have preferred her on this particular point – his job – to be a little less definite.

'By the way, Etta,' said Bonny, 'you haven't done your Christmas list yet. We know about the sparkly collar for Weech, but you haven't told us anything else . . .'

'Well, yes,' said Etta. 'That's because I didn't want to get all my presents delivered by drone. I was hoping . . .' She trailed off.

'For the real Santa to deliver them . . .' whispered her dad to her mum.

'Dad – that was a rubbish whisper. I can hear you. And, basically, well: *yes*.'

He nodded but looked a bit pained.

'I just like the idea of Christmas like it used to be,' said Etta. 'Like Grandma used to tell me about. It sounds better than Winterzone's Christmas!'

'Etta,' he said. 'Come on – it's my *job*. It's not fair that you're always having a go at me about it.' He paused. Etta looked at him. She felt something that she knew she shouldn't, but sometimes she couldn't help thinking that her dad was a bit of a wimp. She turned away.

Gary took a deep breath. 'And also, I was hoping . . .'

He stopped.

'What?' said Etta, turning back.

'Oh, it doesn't matter.'

'What, Dad?'

'Well, work is looking for a kid to do Perfect Present Please this year, and . . .'

He trailed off. Etta stared at him.

'Why would I get chosen for that?'

'Just trust me,' said her dad. 'You would.'

Etta raised an eyebrow. She didn't quite know what to think. She was not fond of Winterzone's version of Christmas. She hankered for something else, something vanished. But she was still a kid, and kids like presents. As, to be fair, do adults. But not as much as kids. She opened her mouth to reply, without really knowing what to say. But her dad spoke first.

'Also, it's not true that we – that Winterzone – have ruined Christmas!'

Ding-dong, went the doorbell suddenly. Which Etta was quite pleased about, as, being a definite person, she didn't like not quite knowing what to say.

Actually, it went 'Ding-dong merrily on high'. Or at least it played the music to that song in a plinky-plinky way. Except it seemed to be missing the last note. So it went plink-plink plink-plink-plink plink . . . nothing.

'I'll get that,' said Bonny, leaving the room. Then she paused at Etta's door. 'We got that doorbell from Xmasmart, by the way,' she said.

CHAPTER 6

XMX deliveries

I have to go,' said Gary to Etta. He was putting his coat on. 'But please, Etta, just . . . help me out here. I get it. You don't like Winterzone's Christmas. But perhaps just . . . think about the Perfect Present thing. You can ask for anything you want!'

He came over and kissed her on the top of her head. Etta looked up at him. Her face softened a little. She didn't like it when her dad had a big

'Pardon?' she said.

'Sorry,' he said. 'I thought you were bringing me that box. To pick up and deliver somewhere.' He came over and looked down into it. He kept on looking down into it for what seemed like a long time.

'Yes,' he said quietly. 'That looks like it's for me.'

Etta hurriedly put the lid on her box.

'No!' she said firmly. 'This stays with me.'

She looked up at the delivery guy as she said it. He was wearing a red uniform and a small white cap. The name of the company he worked for was XMX. He hadn't shaved, so his face had quite a lot of stubbly grey and white hair on it. Underneath his overalls, she noticed he had clearly eaten, in his life, a few big dinners.

His face, as he looked up, appeared very sad. Etta frowned. There was something . . . familiar about him. But before she could think further about this, he seemed to shake his sadness off and smiled. His teeth were whiter than she would have expected, and his smile broader.

'Oh well!' he said, turning away. 'Bye!'

Etta watched him leave.

'He seemed a bit weird,' said Gary.

'Oh, you think anyone who doesn't wear a suit and speak in statistics is weird,' said Bonny.

'That is totally unfair!' said Gary. And they were off having another one of their rows.

Etta noticed, on the floor near the door, a card. She bent down towards it. It was the kind that delivery people leave when they've come to drop off a package but you're out. *The man must have dropped it*, she thought. She picked it up. It had the address of the XMX depot on it.

Hmm, thought Etta.

CHAPTER 7

Ho ho no

'Of course he wasn't *Santa!*' said Monty.

'How do you know?' asked Etta.

'Well, for a number of reasons. Shall I list them?'

Monty was Etta's friend at her school, Bracket Wood. She often sat with him, as she was doing now, in the dining hall when they were having lunch. She liked him a lot, even though he was always very convinced he was right about everything. He also wore a shirt and tie and jacket, which no one had to do at Bracket Wood.

'No,' said Etta, who knew how long Monty's lists were. But it was too late. Monty had raised his hand and was pointing to his thumb with the index finger of his other hand.

'One. Santa lives in the North Pole, not round here.

'Two. Santa only comes away from the North Pole on Christmas Eve. Yesterday, when you met this delivery guy, was the nineteenth of December.

'Three. Santa wears a big red Santa suit with white fur trim. Not an XMX uniform.

'Four. He arrived at your house via – I'm guessing – a van. Not a sleigh drawn by flying reindeer.

'Five. He—'

'Yes, all right, Monty,' interrupted Etta. 'I get it. But . . . *that* Santa – the one you're talking about—'

'The real one,' said Monty.

Etta smiled. Monty could be a bit annoying but

she liked that he said that. And that he had known that that was what she meant.

'Yes, the real one – *no one* knows where he is now. Because he seems to have vanished. It's like he's . . . retired. Or something.'

'Well, the way I understand it is . . .' Monty paused. He looked over his shoulder and then back again. Then he leaned towards her, across his plate of mashed potatoes (that's what he tended to eat, just mashed potatoes) and lowered his voice. ' . . . Is that Winterzone basically forced him out of the job.'

Etta frowned. 'Where did you hear that?'

Monty sat back. He looked smug. 'I keep my ear to the ground.'

'The internet, then,' said Etta.

'Obviously.'

'Why would they do that?' said Etta.

'He knows where the bodies are buried,' said Monty.

'What does that mean?'

'I'm not sure. I heard a grown-up say it once. But I think the real reason is obvious. Winterzone wanted to take over Christmas. They couldn't have Santa going around saying, "Well, *that's* not right. That's wrong. That's not in the spirit of Christmas, is it? Ho ho *no*—" and stuff like that, could they?'

Etta considered this. Part of Monty being annoying was that he thought he was right about *everything*. And clearly, he thought he was right about Santa and Winterzone here. But the more Etta thought about what he was saying now, the more she thought: *He IS right. That really sounds right.*

'My dad—' said Etta.

'The one who works for Winterzone,' said Monty.

'Yes. Although I only have one dad.'

'Yep. Don't know why I said, "the one".'

'OK. Weird. Anyway, he said he thinks I could be the Perfect Present Please kid this year . . .'

Monty's eyes widened. 'Wow!'

'Yes . . . but I haven't said I will be.'

Monty stared at her. 'Sorry, I think there's something wrong with my hearing. I *heard* you say that even though your dad has told you you could be, you haven't agreed to be the Perfect Present Please kid this year. But that can't be right, can it?'

Etta didn't say anything.

'You know you can ask for *anything*, right? And they *have* to get it for you?'

'Yes, Monty, I know. I'm . . . I'm thinking about it. Meanwhile, can't you come with me? To the depot? Just to see?'

'See what?'

'If . . . if the delivery guy looks like Santa to you.'

Monty frowned. He spooned some more mash into his mouth. 'Do I need to tell you my list again?'

'Don't talk with your mouth full. No. You don't. I get you don't think he's Santa. He probably isn't.

Of course he isn't. But . . . he was a bit mysterious. For a delivery guy. So, I'd like to see.' Etta wondered about something – something that might make Monty come with her. 'And I think you know about stuff . . . You know about most things – you're *right* about most things – so I thought, if you came, I could rely on you to know.'

Monty swallowed a mouthful of potato. He shrugged.

'OK, I'll come with you.'

Etta smiled. Monty might think he was right about most things, but *she* had been right about one thing, which is that he was susceptible to flattery.

CHAPTER 8

The delivery guy in question

'Who?' said Jada. Etta knew Jada was her name, as she (the woman presently manning – womaning, rather – the customer booth at the XMX depot) was wearing a large name badge on top of her red uniform.

Etta looked down at the card that the delivery guy had given her. It didn't have a name on it. It just had the address of the XMX depot. The XMX depot, by the way, was not the loveliest place Etta had ever been. Etta's family were not rich, and so she hadn't been to that many lovely places, but even given that, the XMX depot – an old, rectangular building at the end of a narrow alley off Etta's local high road, with cracks in most of its windows and a prevailing smell that had without doubt an element of wee to it – wasn't in the top one hundred.

'I don't know his name,' said Etta.

'No idea at all what it might be?' said Jada.

Etta frowned. There was something – a possible name – she wanted to say, but she knew that, if she did, Jada would think she was mad. 'He was just an XMX delivery guy who came round to our flat a few days ago. He gave us this card . . .'

Etta handed it through the dip under the glass screen between her and Jada. Standing next to her, Monty watched on. The card was now very creased and smudged with fingerprints. Jada held it up, at some distance away from herself, to read it.

'Yes,' she said. 'This *is* the address of our depot. But normally people come here to pick up parcels that couldn't be delivered because they were out. Our guys leave these cards to let them know, but I can't see any reference to a parcel that wasn't delivered . . .'

'No,' said Monty, barging past Etta. A small queue of people had now formed behind them: a man holding a baby in a sling on his chest, and, behind him, an extremely old-looking lady with a hearing aid and a walking frame. 'We've already explained. He *wasn't* trying to deliver a parcel to Etta. He was trying to deliver a parcel to another address. But then he dropped this card. And we decided to come here to find out . . . a bit more information about him.'

Jada's eyes narrowed at Monty. 'What sort of "*more* information"?'

Monty blinked at her. 'I think we are only prepared

to discuss that with the delivery guy in question, thank you very much.'

Jada took a deep breath. She tossed the XMX card back through the dip beneath her window. 'How old are you?'

Monty blinked at her. 'Eleven.'

'I get the sense,' she said, 'that despite being only eleven, you think you know everything. You think you're right about everything.'

'Well, that's insightful of you,' said Monty. 'I do, yes.'

Now it was Jada's turn to blink. She was clearly a little surprised that he seemed to have taken what she said as a compliment. 'Well, if you know everything, my eleven-year-old sir, perhaps *you* can tell me, since your friend couldn't, this delivery guy's *name*? That is all I'm asking.'

Again, there was a word – a name – that Etta desperately wanted to say. It was on the tip of her tongue. She had to bite her tongue, in fact, not to say it.

'I don't know his name either,' said Monty.

'Oh,' said Jada. 'Right. So turns out you *don't* know everything.'

'Excuse me,' said the man with the baby. 'Um . . . I don't mean to be rude . . . but can we hurry up?' He gestured to the baby, who was making some strange faces. Like babies make sometimes. The kind that makes you think: *Why is that baby making that face? That kind of STRAINING face?* And then, soon after, you know why.

Jada considered the two children, who were looking a bit sad. Well, Etta was looking sad; Monty was looking more confused, perhaps at the idea that it turns out he actually *didn't* know something – and Jada's face softened.

'Look. So. You don't know this guy's name. We've established that. But what did he look like?'

Etta said: 'He looks like . . .' She felt the word, the name, rise again in her head. It was so hard not to say it. Jada was looking at her encouragingly. Monty, however, was looking at her in whatever the opposite of encouragingly was. He was frowning and shaking his head.

But she felt like she wanted to say it anyway. She felt like saying it out loud would somehow bring him – the person whose name this was – into being.

'He looks like . . .' she repeated. 'He looks like . . .

'Waaaaah!' screamed the baby. *'Waaah waaah!'*

'Oh my Lordy Lord Lordies!' said the old lady, loudly. 'What is that terrible smell?! I say, what is that *terrible* smell? It's like a very fat pig that's eaten only rotten eggs has just burped!'

'Um . . .' said the man. 'It's OK, baby. Shh, shhhh . . . Do you have a toilet here?' he asked Jada.

'I think I'm going to faint!' moaned the old lady. 'Where is it coming from? I've never smelt anything so horrible in my life and I've lived for ninety-four years!'

' . . . San—' said Etta, trying to make herself heard over the shouting.

'Who?' said Jada.

'San—!'

'OMG!' said Jada, putting her hand up to her nose and mouth. 'She's right. Sorry!' She put up a sign that said 'WINDOW CLOSED' and turned away, quickly making her way into a back room, where she could be heard coughing and spluttering.

'No – but I wanted to tell you: HE LOOKED LIKE—' said Etta.

And the next thing she knew, she was outside the depot.

CHAPTER 9

An ancient skunk that died

Monty was breathing very heavily. In through his nose, loudly, and out through his mouth, also loudly.

'Are you OK?' said Etta.

Monty gestured with his hand, a wave that could have meant 'yes' or 'absolutely not'. He didn't seem to be able to speak.

'Sorry, I was talking, so I didn't breathe in through my nose, so I didn't smell—'

'An ancient skunk that died! IT WAS WORSE THAN THAT!'

'I'm sorry. Look, I'm *sorry.*'

They looked round, to see that the old lady was leaving the depot, but not before continuing to berate the young man with the baby. At least the baby was looking a bit happier.

'OK,' said Monty, gasping. 'I think I can talk now.'

'Oh good.'

'Sorry for pushing you outside,' said Monty. 'It was partly because of the smell, but also because I didn't want you to say what you were going to say.'

'What, "Santa"?' asked Etta.

'Yes?'

Etta frowned. Because it wasn't Monty who said that.

'Who said that?' said Monty. Which frankly is another clue that the *Yes?* had not been said by him.

Etta looked round. There was a concreted area

round the back of the depot. From her point of view, it seemed to be just red vans parked there. But then she heard a cough. She glanced at Monty. Monty glanced back at her. The sky was getting darker. They had gone to the depot on the way home from school – it was only a short detour from her normal walk home – and Etta knew her mum would be beginning to be worried about her. But she moved towards the sound.

CHAPTER 10

Papa Noël

Sitting on a small red crate round the back of the depot was a man. He was in the shadow of the brick wall, so quite hard to see. Etta squinted at him. She was pretty sure it was the man who had come round to her flat. He had more stubble today: it was becoming a beard.

'Hello?' she said. The wee smell was stronger round this side of the depot. She very much hoped that this wasn't because of the man on the crate.

'Did you say "yes"?'

'What?' said the man, not looking up.

'When I said . . . that name. Did you say "yes"?'

'What name?'

Etta felt a bit embarrassed again. But Monty suddenly appeared next to her and just said it out loud:

'Santa!'

Now the man looked up. As he did so, a light came on. Not a dazzling light from a star, or an amazing burst of glitter from nowhere, but a security light on the side of the XMX depot wall. It did reveal him, though, to definitely be the same delivery guy who had come round to Etta's flat.

It also revealed him – because now his cap was off – to have white hair, along with his white semi-beard. It shone against the light, and there seemed to be a small bit of what looked to Etta like egg yolk in his semi-beard.

'No,' he said, and put his face down again.

'You did!' said Monty. 'You *definitely* did. She said, "Santa?" And you said, "Yes?"'

'I didn't,' said Delivery Guy.

'You did,' said Monty.

'Didn't.'

'Did.'

'Didn't.'

'OK,' said Etta, sensing that she might be dealing here with *two* people who always thought they were right. 'Just stop a minute. Are you the guy who came round to my flat the other day? And gave us this card?'

She held it up. Delivery Guy stared at her for a moment. He got up, his knee bones creaking as he did so.

'Urrggggghhh . . .' he said.

'Are you OK?'

'What? Yes. I make that noise when I get up. You

will do too when you get to my age. Well, you won't get to my age, but . . .' He trailed off.

'Sorry, what?' said Etta.

'Nothing.'

He took the card from her and stared at it.

'Might be . . .' he said. 'I go to a lot of places. I'm a delivery guy.'

'Look,' said Monty. 'Can we cut to the chase? She thinks you're Santa.'

'Well,' said Etta, 'I don't know if I exactly think tha—'

Monty raised a hand to stop her talking. 'So. Are you Santa?'

Delivery Guy frowned. 'Who?'

'Who?' said Monty. '*Who?* You know. Father Christmas. Saint Nicholas. Kris Kringle. Papa Noël.'

'Sorry, what?' said Etta.

'That's what he's called in Egypt.' Monty turned back to the man. 'Baba Chaghaloo.'

'What?'

'That's what he's called in Afghanistan.' He paused, and raised a finger, as if noting something to himself. 'Shall I just add the information after the name? Might be quicker. Deda Mraz. Serbia.' He turned to Etta. 'It means "Chilling Grandpa" or "Old Man Winter". He turned back towards the man. 'Hotei-Osho!'

'Bless you,' said Etta.

'No, it's the name of a Buddhist monk in Japan who's the equivalent of Santa Claus. Sinterklaas . . .'

'That just sounds like "Santa Claus" said in a different accent,' said Etta.

'Dutch, to be exact.'

'Goodness, Monty. You really do know a lot of stuff,' she said. 'Some of it not really relevant to what we're doing here . . .'

'Right,' said Delivery Guy. 'Anyway, I'm not. Any of those people.'

'Well, it's all the *same* person. Under a lot of different names,' said Etta.

'How interesting,' the man said. 'I have to go.'

He started to walk off. Monty seemed to have an idea. 'Where to?' he said quickly.

'The North Pole,' said Delivery Guy, without turning round. Then he suddenly did turn, and said, with one of his palms placed on his cheek: 'Oh dear! What a giveaway! You've caught me out! You are such a clever tiny Sherlock Holmes! Clearly, I *am* Santa!'

'You're being sarcastic now, aren't you?' said Etta.

'I am,' he said.

'Ho ho ho,' said Monty.

CHAPTER 11

Definitely not Santa!

'**N**o,' said Monty. They were walking away from the depot.

'No,' said Etta. 'I agree. You're right. Again.'

'Well, yes,' said Monty.

'I mean, you are, definitely. He's *definitely* not Santa.'

'He's just a delivery guy.'

'He is. It was a stupid idea.' Etta sighed. She stopped walking. 'I'm going to be late. I'd better let my mum know.' She took out her phone. She was allowed to have a phone, even though she was only eleven, because her mum was often at work and her dad didn't live with them, so her mum had given it to her because she couldn't always pick her up from school.

She selected the Videocall option of the phone.

'I guess . . .' she said, while she was waiting for her mum to answer, 'I may as well tell her what my Christmas list is now. Because I guess I do still want some presents. And I guess – I've said "guess" a lot now, haven't I?'

Monty nodded.

'I guess they may as well be delivered by drones or whatever in the usual way.'

Monty nodded again. He felt a bit sad for Etta. But although he did like to think of himself as knowing lots of stuff, he didn't know what to do to make the world – and Christmas – be the way his friend wanted it to be.

Etta held her phone up. It seemed to be having difficulty finding a signal. But suddenly a face – not her mum's – appeared on the screen. It was a kindly, smiling face. Or at least, that was the impression the face was *trying* to give.

'Hello, Etta.'

'Uh . . . who are you?' she said.

'Call me Bry,' said the face.

CHAPTER 12
Tech-knowledgey

'What's going on?' said Etta, stopping in the street.

'Etta! Here's the thing. It's OK. It's so OK,' said Bry. 'Look! Here's your dad!'

The phone image moved. It seemed like the phone was not being held by the man speaking. The image turned round to show a very large room – more like a huge hall than a room. Etta saw her dad with some other grown-ups standing around him. He was low down, stuck in some kind of very big beanbag.

'Um . . .' said her dad, shifting himself up towards the camera.

'Yes, there he is,' said Bry. The camera turned back round to him, Bry. 'Anyway, here's the thing.'

'You say that quite a lot,' said Etta.

'It's my thing. To say, "Here's the thing." So, here's the thing, E – can I call you E?'

'No,' said Etta. 'No one calls me E.'

'OK,' he said chucklingly. 'Well, Etta. Sorry to intercept your call—'

'Dad – did you let them do this?'

'No, E,' said her dad's voice, off-camera.

'I thought no one called you that,' said Bry.

'OK, my dad calls

me that,' said Etta. 'And my mum. But you're not my dad or mum.'

'Um . . . anyway, E . . .' came her dad's voice hurriedly. 'I didn't know this, but turns out that Winterzone have—'

'The ability to intercept all phone calls in . . . what radius is it now, Raisa?' said Bry, his face moving away from the screen a little.

'The world,' said a strange female voice. It sounded like it was the person holding the camera.

'Oh! Great!'

'Is that great?' said Monty. 'Hacking?'

'Hi! Monty, right?' said Bry, his eyes moving towards him.

'Um . . . yes.'

'Monty Cohen, of 41A Shackleton Avenue. Eleven years, three months old. Most visited sites: Infopedia, Knowledge dot com, SmartAlec dot net . . .' said the female voice behind the phone.

'Hey! How do you know all that?' said Monty.

Etta looked at her friend. 'You don't sound that unhappy about it . . .'

'No, I'm just interested in how anyone gets to *know* that much.'

'Tech, Monty,' said Bry. 'I actually call it tech-knowledgey.'

'That's just what it's called,' said Monty.

'No, but I'm spelling "knowledgey" with a K.'

'Knology?' said Monty. 'But that *isn't* how you spell it.'

'No, I'm spelling it like "knowled—" You know what? Forget it. Here's the thing, which is the thing. Yes, we know everything. And so we also know, because we have access to all CCTV cameras, especially all CCTV cameras around Christmas delivery depots, where you've both just been, and what you've been saying.' Bry's smile seemed to grow bigger but somehow, now, talk with her. She didn't like that he worked for Winterzone. But she did love him. She understood that a lot of what he said about Christmas and Winterzone wasn't really his fault, that he had to say it.

'OK, Dad. I'll do my best.'

They went out towards the hallway. Bonny was talking to a delivery guy.

'No, that's not ours . . .' she was saying.

'What's happening?' said Gary.

'Oh, this gentleman's just got a little confused. It's a delivery for another flat,' continued Bonny. She pointed out the door. 'Number Eight. It's just down the corridor.'

'Is that for me?' said the delivery guy.

Etta looked up. The delivery guy was ignoring Bonny and pointing at Etta's box, which she was still holding. The lid was off. Her eyes reflected the sparkling tinsel and bauble inside.

not kinder. 'And we at Winterzone are really wondering why you've been doing that.'

CHAPTER 13

It's not a mantra!

'Bryan . . .' said Gary, clambering up somehow out of the beanbag.

'Bry!' said Bry.

'Yes – anyway . . .' He came towards Bry. Raisa glided – it was almost like she didn't have feet – between them. She stared at him impassively. Gary backed away a little. In a quieter voice he said:

'I'm not really, uh, comfortable with you – um – threatening my daughter.'

'Hey. I'm not threatening her. Am I threatening her, guys?'

'NO!' said Hamnet, Fester and CWX25.

'YES!' said the other Hamnet.

'Shh, you stupid cockatoo,' said Hamnet.

'I am not, Gary,' said Bry. He looked closely into the phone, an extremely sleek-looking one that was indeed being held up by Raisa. 'You understand, don't you, Etta?'

Etta's face, on the screen, frowned. 'Not really . . .'

'Well, let me explain. Winterzone. It's a platform. It's not a publisher. It's a platform.'

'I don't know what you're talking about,' said Etta.

'I haven't finished explaining. What I mean is: we are a place through which Christmas . . . flows.'

'A place through which Christmas flows,' intoned Fester, Hamnet, Hamnet and Raisa. It was another mantra.

'A place – yeah, yeah! – through which Christmas flows!' sang CWX25.

'Is that actually a song?' whispered Fester.

'Don't think so. I think his wiring may have got a bit crossed,' said Gary. 'He has been malfunctioning for a while . . .'

'Look, can you just *leave it*, Gary!' said Hamnet.

'So, it's all good,' continued Bry. 'There's no right or wrong. There are no winners and losers at Winterzone.'

'No winners and losers at Winterzone!' said all the others, like a chorus.

'As long as everything's . . . Christmassy. Right?'

'Still not with you, Bry,' said Etta. 'Dad – is this really your boss?'

'Er, yes,' said Gary.

'Not "boss",' said Bry. 'Everyone here is on the same level.'

'Everyone here,' said everyone, 'is on the s—'

'IT'S NOT A MANTRA!' shouted Bry. He closed his eyes, and took a deep breath.

'In . . . .Out . . . In . . . Out . . .' said Raisa.

'Yes, all right, Raisa, I know how to breathe. My point is, Etta, I brought your dad in here because I wanted to show you – and him – that this is a safe space. And, in this safe space, I can say to you that we at Winterzone are *really* not sure why you and your friend Monty Cohen might want to go to an XMX depot and ask a lot of strange questions to the people who work there, and then a lot of frankly even stranger questions to one of the delivery guys round the back. BUT – and I want to be very clear about this – I'm just putting that out there. I'm just saying it. We are very committed to free speech, which means I can say that to you, and you can push back to me, and tell me what you think.'

'What I think . . .?'

'Yes. You can tell me what you think. Maybe as

part of that you can tell me what exactly was in YOUR mind, and what exactly YOU were thinking by going there and asking those questions.'

'Hey, Bry . . . I'm also really not comfortable with you asking my daughter these things,' said Gary.

Raisa, who was still standing between Gary and Bry, blinked at him. But Bry said: 'OK. I get that. Of course.' He gestured to Raisa, who moved the phone so that it was filming Gary. 'Perhaps you can ask her.'

'Pardon?' said Gary.

'Perhaps *you* can ask your daughter why she went to the XMX depot and spoke to the guy round the back. If you're not comfortable with *me* doing it.'

Gary looked lost. He looked into the camera. His daughter's face looked out at him. Raisa pushed the camera closer to him with one hand. Her other hand seemed to be gripping tighter than ever on to her orange bag with the green clasps.

'I . . .' he began. 'Etta, I . . .'

'It's OK, Dad,' said Etta.

'It is?' said Gary.

'Really. It is. I don't want to cause you any problems at work. I'm sorry we went to the XMX depot. I'm sorry we asked the guy round the back some strange questions. It was just a stupid idea. A stupid little kid's idea. I realise that now. Don't worry, Dad . . . and, Bry – everyone at Winterzone – I won't be doing anything like that again. OK?'

Gary looked at her. He felt relieved.

'Thank you, Etta,' he said. Raisa took the phone and trained it back on Bry.

'Yes!' said Bry. 'Thank you, from all of us here.' He put his hands together, palms upwards. 'You're clearly a great girl. Who understands what's important. And who also . . . maybe . . . would be a great candidate for Perfect Present Please!'

A cheer – a 'YES!' – went up from Hamnet, Hamnet and Fester.

Etta didn't say anything.

Raisa clicked off the phone. Gary returned his gaze to Bry, who was looking back at him with his most kindly smile. He looked at Gary for a long time, maintaining eye contact the whole time. Gary looked back at Bry, wondering when it would be OK for him to look away, and really hoping it would be soon as it was just getting unbearably awkward.

'Group hug,' said Bry eventually.

'YAY! GROUP HUG!' said Fester, Hamnet and Hamnet. They all – even Hamnet the cockatoo, who fluttered his wings at the group, his best attempt at a hugging gesture – came together round Gary and Bry and hugged. All except Raisa, who just watched calmly. And also CMX25, who had walked away in the wrong direction and was hugging the beanbag.

CHAPTER 14

Full steam ahead

'So . . .' said Monty, as Etta clicked off the phone. 'That's it? We've given up on your idea? Standard drone Santavatar Winterzone-controlled Christmas full-steam ahead?'

'Thing is, Monty . . .' said Etta, 'I was about to give up. I *had* given up. But ask yourself a question: *why* would Winterzone be so worried about us going to XMX and asking that delivery guy if he was Santa? *Why* would they be so keen to shut us down?'

Monty turned away.

'What? Come on, Monty! You're the guy who's supposed to know everything! Surely you can work out what that means?!'

'Yes, I can. And surely you can work out why I'm walking this way – why, in fact, we should both go straight back to speak again to—' He put both his hands over his mouth, like people do when they shout

sometimes, to create a kind of megaphone effect, although Monty could've told you, because he knew a lot of stuff, that doing that doesn't make your voice any louder, but still, he was doing it anyway.

' . . . SANTA!'

PART TWO:
STILL THE NEAR FUTURE

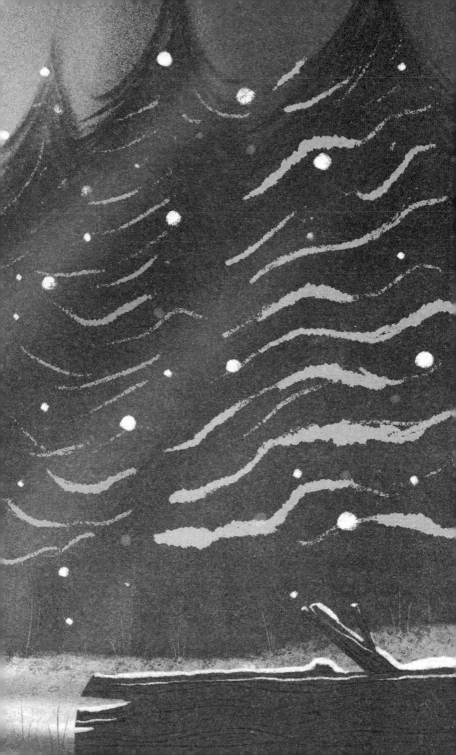

CHAPTER 15

Stake-out

Monty and Etta went straight back to the XMX depot, but by the time they got there it had shut. Luckily, next day was an inset day at school, so they were off. Which meant they could return once more to XMX.

Monty had an idea, which was that instead of marching in again and asking the delivery guy questions, this time they do what he called a 'stake-out'. A stake-out, he explained, was when two detectives – 'either police or maybe private detectives', he insisted on making clear – sit in a car and eat doughnuts and drink coffee while secretly watching someone in their house or at work, to find out some secret thing about them.

'We don't have a car,' said Etta. 'And I don't drink coffee.'

'No,' said Monty. 'But I do have some doughnuts. My auntie makes them. Especially at this time of year . . .'

He produced a paper bag. She looked inside. The doughnuts were small (there were four of them) but they looked delicious – bursting with jam and covered in sugar.

'OK!' she said, taking one out and stuffing it in her mouth.

An hour and a half later, there were no doughnuts left, both of their hands were sticky from sugar, and there had been no sign of anyone except a couple of customers picking up parcels from the XMX depot. Monty and Etta were sitting on a bench on the opposite side of the road, and it wasn't feeling much like fun.

'Stake-outs look much more exciting in the movies,' said Monty.

'Well, maybe that's because they have warm cars to sit in. And coffee,' said Etta.

'Yes, and it always seems like an endless supply of doughnuts. Rather than four. Shall we give up?'

Etta nodded. It was nearly lunchtime. And the doughnuts had somehow ended up making her hungrier. She was just starting to think about how her mum might be making spaghetti for lunch when Monty said, 'Wait! Is that him . . .?'

Etta looked over. She could see a flash of white beard, under a red scarf. He was also wearing a red – she really wondered if these were clues – cap.

'It is. I'm sure.'

'Let's follow him!'

'Really?' said Etta.

'Yes. That's the point of the stake-out. What else would be the point? It can't just be about doughnuts!'

'Right,' she said, but Monty was already up the street, and chasing Delivery Guy.

CHAPTER 16

Snow

'**W**here's he going *now*?' whispered Etta. They had been following Delivery Guy for nearly an hour. He had walked through the High Street. It was empty, and a lot of the shops were shut. Etta remembered that it didn't use to be, especially this close to Christmas. She had dim memories of going shopping with Grandma Jo, one Christmas long ago. All the shops had been open late, full of people going in and out. The street had been so decked with lights that it felt like thousands of fireflies were hovering above her and Grandma in the night air.

The emptiness now did make it quite difficult for Monty and Etta to follow Delivery Guy without him seeing them because there would be no one to hide behind if he turned round. But then again, he didn't turn round. He just trudged slowly on and on.

Finally, he took a turn into a road that led into a park. Both Etta and Monty knew the park well – their school sometimes came there for sports days. But then Delivery Guy took a turn into some trees, into a kind of foresty bit of the park that they didn't usually go into.

They stopped and looked at each other.

'Shall we go in?' said Etta.

'We probably shouldn't . . .' said Monty. 'I don't know this bit of the park. We might get lost.'

'Well. You know best,' said Etta.

He nodded. There was a short pause. And then they both headed towards the trees.

Although it was the middle of the day, parts of the forest area were quite dark. Sunlight gleamed through the tops of the trees, but, on the ground, Etta and Monty were almost completely in shadow.

'Which way did he go?' said Etta.

Monty shook his head. His knowing-everythingness was definitely looking fragile.

'Is there not a way we can track him? I'm sure I've seen that on nature programmes,' said Etta.

'That's for animals,' said Monty. 'You track them via their droppings.'

'Their . . .?'

'Poo. I'd prefer not to do that with a human man.'

'OK . . . then we've lost him . . . Oh!' she said.

'Wow,' said Monty.

They were both looking towards a section of the forest in front of them.

This was an age in which, even in December, snow didn't fall. People were aware of snow, through stories and films and computer simulations created by Winterzone, but they didn't see it for themselves. Something had changed in the climate. So although people got to see snow on the screen, they didn't feel it – the silence, and the calmness, the way that life shifts softly with the light, with the gentle covering of the earth with white.

Certainly, Etta and Monty had never felt it.

But they felt it now.

CHAPTER 17

Santa's actual grotto

'This is amazing!' shouted Etta, running towards it. It wasn't the deepest snow, but it was deep enough to jump into and roll around in. It was even deep enough for Monty, as if he'd been doing it every winter of his life, to clump together snowballs and chuck them at Etta while she was rolling around, and for her to do the same back to him. Looking up, it seemed to them like the snow had just formed, somehow, on the branches of the trees and fallen to the ground from there.

'It's weird,' said Monty, sitting up. 'It's like it's just this bit of the forest that has been snowed on . . .'

'Huh?' said Etta.

'Well, it's like when we were standing over there it wasn't snowing – and it still isn't – but it is over here.'

'Hey!' said Etta, not that bothered about the

weirdness of the weather. 'Look! Snow means . . .'

She got up and ran towards . . .

'Footprints!' said Monty.

'So we don't need poo!!'

'Pardon?'

'Droppings!'

'Oh . . . No!' said Monty.

The tracks led off into the distance. 'Come on,' said Etta, 'before they melt!'

They ran, following the line of the footprints. They were easy to follow. One thing about Delivery Guy was that, as we know, he was not a small man, so his footprints were deep, very deep – as deep as the quite-deep snow went. Etta and Monty ran together, looking down. It was like the line of footprints was an arrow, showing the way to go.

The line curved away behind a particularly dense clump of trees. They followed it round.

'Perhaps . . .' said Etta breathlessly, 'perhaps round here, at the end of the tracks, there'll be a grotto! Santa's actual grotto! Perhaps he's moved it from the North Pole to . . .'

'Bracket Wood Donkey Sanctuary,' said Monty.

'Well, that's a bit more specific than I meant.'

'No,' said Monty. 'Stop looking at the footprints. Look up.'

She did. In front of them was a splintered and broken wooden fence. In the middle of the fence was a splintered and broken wooden house – well, more of a shed really. With a sign on it that said 'BRACKET WOOD DONKEY SANCTUARY'.

CHAPTER 18
Bracket Wood Donkey Sanctuary

've been over this. He *has* to have carrots.'

'They don't *have* carrots. I tell you this every time.'

'It's a *donkey* sanctuary. Donkeys are always eating carrots!'

'No, they're not. Only in cartoons. Or in stories about whether it's better to get mules – which aren't donkeys anyway – to move along a road with carrots or sticks.'

'That's definitely carrots!'

'Yes, but they don't normally actually *get* carrots. They get hay, or grass. Which is what the food is here as well!'

Etta and Monty watched this conversation from behind the door of the Bracket Wood Donkey Sanctuary. There were lots of holes in that door, so watching – and hearing – it wasn't difficult.

The conversation was between Delivery Guy, who was doing the thing of insisting that there should be carrots, and another man, dressed in green overalls and a red bobble cap, who was doing the 'there are no carrots' thing. This other man also had a beard, but it was shorter than Delivery Guy's, which today seemed like it had grown to quite a flowing length. And this other man's beard was ginger, and he was also considerably smaller than Delivery Guy. They were standing inside the wooden house – well, more of a shed really – but behind them was a large stable door, flung open on to a grassy area beyond. It was more of a field than a forest and was covered in snow. In the distance, standing around and looking as if nothing in the world was ever likely to bother them, were two donkeys.

'Who are they talking about?' whispered Etta, taking her eye away from the hole she was peeping through.

'Him,' said Monty, who had stayed looking through his. Etta put her eye back. Through the peephole she could see, clopping into view behind the man in green overalls, another donkey.

'That donkey?'

'You can't see through your peephole that well, can you?'

Etta adjusted her sightline. It was true, she couldn't see the whole picture. When she crouched down a bit, though, and looked up, so as to have a view that was of a little higher up, she could see that it was a donkey . . . with antlers. So not a donkey at all, in fact.

'It's a reindeer!' she screamed. 'It must be . . . It is . . . It's RUDOL—'

'No, it isn't,' said Delivery Guy, opening the door. 'And can you two *please* go away!'

CHAPTER 19

Clever tiny Sherlock Holmes

Monty gave Etta a look that had quite a strong sense of 'maybe *screaming* about the reindeer was a bad idea?' But Etta didn't even return his glance. She looked up at the delivery guy, and at the man in green overalls, who had appeared next to him, drew herself up to her full height – which incidentally was about that of Green Overalls Man – and just came out with it:

'IT IS. It's Rudolph. Stop pretending. You're a

delivery guy. Who wears red clothes. With a beard. You've got a big, round belly.'

'Rude,' said Delivery Guy.

'Well, you have,' said Etta. 'In terms of what I'm saying, that's a good thing.'

Delivery Guy raised his eyes up to heaven. 'And what exactly *are* you saying?'

'Wait a minute – I haven't finished my list of clues. You live in this place, where it's snowing, which it doesn't seem to do anywhere else in the world any more. You have a small friend . . .'

'Rude,' said Green Overalls Man.

'Again, not necessarily in this context,' said Etta. 'A small friend, as I say, who's dressed in green. Like an *elf*. And, most importantly, you seem to be looking after a *reindeer*.' She looked beyond the two men, towards the field, where the reindeer stood. Its face was fairly blank, as, to be honest, reindeer faces normally are. 'Why would an ordinary delivery

guy be looking after a reindeer? Tell me that, Mister Not-Santa-At-All-Why-Would-You-Think-That-Get-Out-Of-Here!'

'Well,' said the delivery guy. 'That is all very interesting. I could point out one or two anomalies . . .'

'Annamolly'swhatnow?' asked Etta.

'Anomalies. It means things that don't work with what you're saying,' said Monty.

'For example, tell me this . . .' said the delivery guy, bending down towards the children. He raised an arm and pointed behind him. 'Where's his red nose, eh? Where's that?'

'It is *quite* red,' said the man in green, touching his nose.

'No—'

'I blow it a lot. It's cold here. Cos of the snow.'

'NO!' said the delivery guy, pointing towards the back field. 'NOT YOUR NOSE! THE REINDEER'S!'

They all looked out at the field. Etta squinted.

It was true. The reindeer's nose was not red. It was brown. With spots of white. Like reindeer noses are.

Etta looked back at the delivery guy. He had stood up, with his arms folded. He had a very *'Aha!'* expression on his face. A very *'put that in your pipe and smoke it'* expression. A very *'I've won – do close the door on your way out'* expression.

'Yeah,' said the man in green overalls, turning round from a long look at the reindeer. 'But that's Prancer. You know that's Prancer. He doesn't have a red nose.' He turned to the children, gestured with his thumb at the delivery guy, and whispered – but quite loudly, in a way that meant everyone could hear – 'I sometimes worry that he can't remember anything any more!'

There was a long pause. The delivery guy uncrossed his arms. Monty and Etta crossed theirs. It was their turn to assume *'Aha!'* faces.

'Oh dear,' said Monty. 'What a giveaway! We've

caught you out! We are two such clever tiny Sherlock Holmeses! Clearly, you are . . . Santa!'

There was another pause. Eventually, the delivery guy shrugged. 'Ho ho ho,' said Santa.

CHAPTER 20

Bushy Evergreen

'**B**ut you can't tell *anyone!*' Santa said.

'Why not?' said Etta.

'He's signed a contract . . .' said the small man in green overalls. 'Which includes an NDA. Oh, and by the way, well spotted. I *am* an elf.' He put his hand out. 'Bushy Evergreen. Nice to meet you.'

Monty shook hands with the elf.

'What's an NDA?' said Etta.

'A non-disclosure agreement.'

'A non-discoball-agriwhattynow?'

'It means,' said Santa, sighing heavily, 'that I've legally agreed never to tell anyone that I'm Santa.'

'Or indeed,' said Bushy, 'to perform any Santa-like duties, to include all or part of: making lists of naughty slash nice children, riding a flying sleigh laden with presents, sliding down chimneys, depositing said presents underneath Christmas trees, and saying the word "ho" three times.'

'No, I *am* allowed to do that. I got an exemption. That's why I've been saying it.'

'Oh, OK – yes, sorry, that is in the small print.'

'Um . . .' said Monty, 'are you his elf lawyer?'

'Yes. OK, I didn't train as one,' said Bushy. 'But I learned what I need to get by off the internet – well, what *he* needs to get by. It's easy enough now that I don't spend much time present-wrapping . . .'

'Why did you sign all that?' said Etta, to Santa.

'Good question,' said the elf lawyer.

'Oh, do shut up, Evergreen.'

'He's become much grouchier since he stopped working,' whispered Bushy to Etta and Monty. 'And he used to be *quite* grouchy then.'

'I can *hear* you!' said Santa.

'Well, if you can *hear*, why don't you answer the question?' said Bushy.

Santa sighed. 'It's a long story.'

'No, it isn't,' said Bushy. 'He basically just got a bit old and tired and fed up with the job . . .'

'Well,' said Santa, looking at Monty and Etta, '*you* try sorting out presents for all the children in the world! And then flying all over the world delivering them. In one night! At my age! When you've spent the rest of the year in the North Pole, which, by the way, is really not a good place for rheumatism. Which I have got, really badly!'

'Yes, well, Winterzone knew something was up with him . . .' said Bushy.

'Yes! I don't know how,' said Santa.

'Did you by any chance message anyone you knew about how you were feeling?'

'Um . . . I might have. I sent an email or two to Mrs Claus, yes. And to Prancer.' He looked at the children. 'He's a *very* clever reindeer, that one.'

'Well, there we are,' said Bushy. 'That's how Winterzone knew. They know about everything that happens on the internet.'

'I didn't really think that Santa—' said Etta. Then she turned to him. '. . . That *you* . . . used the internet . . .'

'All of us elves told him not to get a computer. But would he listen to us?'

'OK, OK!' said Santa. 'I've had enough of this!' He turned round sulkily and stomped back out towards the field towards Prancer, who appeared to have been watching the proceedings calmly.

'Anyway,' continued Bushy, not particularly bothered,

it seemed, by Santa having a strop, 'after Winterzone got wind of how he was feeling, they – Bryan Leaf and some of his people – came to the North Pole (wearing a *lot* of silver padded anoraks) and offered him a deal. They would take over Christmas. He could retire, basically. And Winterzone would look after him . . .'

'They paid him money?!' said Monty, aghast. 'To give up Christmas?!'

'No!' said Bushy. 'They offered him a part-time job delivering presents on a small scale, just to keep his hand in, you know, and—'

'THEY SAID THEY WOULD KEEP THE REAL SPIRIT OF CHRISTMAS ALIVE! THEY LIED TO ME!'

Monty and Etta and Bushy looked over. Santa was leaning against Prancer's flank. In his hand he held a bottle of brown liquid.

'—as much sherry as he could drink,' finished Bushy sadly.

'This is terrible,' said Monty. 'We have to do something!'

Bushy shook his head. 'As long as Winterzone have that contract, there's not much we can do.'

Monty frowned. 'Well . . . what happens if Santa just breaks this contract – and this NDA?'

Bushy looked at him. His face went white. Which was quite a long journey, colour-wise, as its starting position was really rather red.

CHAPTER 21

Something called the internet

'**W**ell? What happens?' asked Etta.

'I don't want to say . . .' Bushy whispered. 'It's so awful.'

'OH, JUST TELL THEM, EVERGREEN!' shouted Santa.

'You can hear me whispering?' said the elf.

'You have a very loud whisper!' said Santa, coming over. His walk did not seem that steady. 'You whisper loudly, like all elves.'

'You really think I should tell them?'

Santa sighed. 'Might as well.' He put his arm round Evergreen, and took another long swig from his bottle of brown liquid. 'I love you, Bushy. Do you know that? I do. You're my best elf.'

'OK,' said Evergreen, pushing him gently away. 'So . . . basically . . . Winterzone have said that if he breaks the contract, they will put it about that . . . that there is no Santa.'

Monty and Etta both frowned at this.

'But . . . that doesn't make sense,' said Etta. 'How can they say there is no Santa if –' she looked over at him: he was dancing now, a small strange jig – 'Santa himself is saying, "Here I am! Santa!"?'

Bushy looked at her. 'You seem not to have heard of something called the internet. Which Winterzone basically own?'

Etta looked at him. 'Have you been eavesdropping on my conversations with my dad?'

'I beg your pardon? Please don't say "elves' droppings".'

'I didn't,' said Etta.

'Anyway. Point is. On the internet now, you can spread any rumour. Any lie. And if you've got enough power and enough reach, lots and *lots* of people will believe that rumour. That lie. And no one has more power and reach on the internet than Winterzone. So, if they decide to say, "Santa doesn't exist," then people will believe it.' Bushy shut his eyes. He whispered – and did his best to reduce the actual volume of it this time: 'I mean, sadly, some people – some children – already don't believe in him.'

'But . . . what about all the Santavatars! They're

all based on Santa!' said Monty.

'They'll just change them to something else. They can do that.'

Monty sighed. Etta looked sad. But then she said:

'Well, he just has to go out there and prove it's him!'

Bushy made a face. They all looked over at Santa. He was lying on the ground, gurgling. The gurgle was sort of to the tune of 'It's the Most Wonderful Time of the Year'. It was hard to tell.

Etta looked back at Bushy. Bushy shrugged. Etta's face changed, away from sadness. Sadness, Etta knew, was not helpful. She shook her head.

'We *can't* just let this happen! Do you know where they keep it? This contract?'

'Well . . . I know where the scary Winterzone woman—' began Bushy.

'Raisa?' asked Etta. 'Bryan Leaf's assistant? The one with the voice like a spy?'

'Yes, her,' said Bushy. 'I know where she put it. In her bag. The one she always carries with her. For all I know, it's still in there.'

Etta smiled. She rubbed her hands together, not against the cold. 'I've got an idea.'

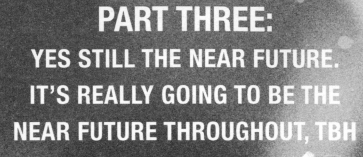

PART THREE:
YES STILL THE NEAR FUTURE.
IT'S REALLY GOING TO BE THE
NEAR FUTURE THROUGHOUT, TBH

CHAPTER 22

CWX25
Mark 2

'm just so pleased you've come, Etta,' said Gary. 'I really didn't think you would.'

'Oh well, Dad,' said Etta, smiling, 'I'm a changed girl.'

Etta and her dad were at Winterzone. Bonny and Jonas were there too. And Monty, who Etta had been allowed to invite. It was Christmas Eve. Or, as Winterzone were in the process of renaming it, Christmas Perfect Present, Please.

'You look wonderful!' said Gary. Etta *was* looking much smarter than she did normally. She never normally, for example, wore a dress. Her hair was never very neat. But now, her hair was combed through and she wore a sparkly silver dress with a matching tiara.

'Well,' said Bonny, 'she allowed me to tidy her up for a change! Although I still don't know why you needed to bring your school bag, Etta.'

Etta glanced down. She had it over her right shoulder.

'Sorry, I just wanted it with me. For . . . emergencies!'

'OK,' said Bonny. 'Well, you still look great. After all, it's not every day that your daughter gets to be the Perfect Present Please girl!'

'No!' said Gary. 'I'm so excited . . . Are you, E?'

'Yes, Daddy!' said Etta.

Gary frowned. Etta never usually called him Daddy. But maybe it was just part of how she'd changed recently. She had come to him a few days ago and said she'd thought about it, and *of course* she would like to be the Perfect Present Please kid, if the offer was still open. *Obviously* she would, she said. What child wouldn't?

He put the Daddy thing out of his mind, as he was desperate to show her, and the rest of the family, something very special before the Perfect Present Please ceremony. They were downstairs, in the basement underneath the main floor of Winterzone. Next to them was a door marked 'TINSELTECH 1'. This was Gary's department. He was one of the few people at Winterzone who actually designed and made real things.

'Listen, everyone,' said Gary. 'We've got ten minutes before it all gets going, so I just want to show you the Super-Sleigh—'

'Is that allowed?' said Bonny.

'It is if I say so!' said Gary. 'I think, if I want to show my family the project I've been working on – for three years! – then who's going to stop me?'

'I'm afraid I am, Gary,' said a voice. It was a smooth, confident, but slightly metallic voice.

They all looked round. Standing in front of the

door of TinselTech 1 was a human-looking robot in a Christmas jumper.

'CWX25?' said Gary.

'Actually, I think you'll find I'm now CWX25 *Mark* 2. I've been upgraded,' said the robot. 'I have been programmed to make sure that the rules are being followed in TinselTech 1 to the letter, including the rule that no one who is not an employee of Winterzone is allowed to see any prototypes that you may or may not be designing in there. That is what I have been programmed to do, Gary. To make sure you stick to that rule.'

Etta, Bonny, Jonas and Monty looked back round, from CWX25 Mark 2 to Gary. Gary looked at them, smiled weakly, and then looked back to the robot.

'Hey . . . CWX25 – come on! Don't be silly. I know we've had a few disagreements . . . but I really want to show my family the Super-Sleigh.' There was a silence. There was a whirring sound, as the robot's head moved slightly from side to side.

'Please accept the rule, Gary,' he said, in his smooth, confident metallic voice.

Gary frowned. He could feel his family's eyes on him. He wasn't, surely, going to be told what to do by a machine?

'CWX25,' he began.

'Mark 2,' said the robot.

'Whatever,' said Gary. 'Please leave the vicinity of TinselTech 1.'

'I can't do that, Gary.'

'Step away from the door, CWX25. Mark 2.'

'You know I can't do that, Gary.'

'OK,' said Gary, and he began to walk round the robot. The robot's head whirred, and his eyes flashed. His hand shot out, and grabbed Gary's shoulder. And then picked Gary up so that his feet were off the floor and wriggling.

'Put me down! CWX25! Mark 2! Put me down!'

'You know I can't do that, Gary!'

There was a whirring sound from within the robot's head. 'Oh, wait a minute . . .' he said. 'I've reprocessed the data, and it turns out I *can* do that. My apologies.' And CWX25 did put Gary down. Dropped him, in fact, in a heap on the floor.

'Ow!' said Gary. 'My head really hurts. And my back! I'm not sure I can get up!'

With a whirr, CWX25's head looked down and smiled. 'Who's malfunctioning now?' he said.

CHAPTER 23

A Bry-te Christmas

'So . . .' said Bry, into his booming head-mic strapped closely to his cheek, 'welcome, everybody – Winterzoners, Winterzoners' families, and all of you watching live on Winterzone dot com and the Winterzone Channel!'

A huge round of applause greeted this, drowning out the sound of one person – it was Monty – asking sarcastically, 'Do you think he's said the word "Winterzone" enough?'

Bry looked around the Snowy Space with his most kindly, smiley expression ever, like he'd been practising kindly smileyness for a month. The Snowy Space was always Christmassy, but tonight it had been ultra-Christmassed – or, at least, ultra-Winterzone Christmassed. The Winterzone logo was everywhere, and, through some very clever CGI techniques, it appeared genuinely to be snowing inside the Snowy Space. All around the Space, against the walls, stood hundreds of Santavatars, waving, like an enormous display of holographic Santa flags.

Bry was speaking from on top of a stage that had been erected at one end of the Snowy Space. In front of him was a large audience. There were many cameras – TV ones and phone ones – trained on the stage. At one side of the stage stood a gospel choir dressed entirely in white robes. They had already sung 'I'm Dreaming of a Bry-te Christmas'.

Monty was in the audience with Bonny and Jonas. A little way apart stood Gary, who, after being dumped on the floor by CWX25, had picked himself up, dusted himself off, and begun to say to the robot, 'Now look here . . .'

But before he'd got any further, Raisa had appeared in the basement, insisted that it was time for Etta to get ready for the Perfect Present Please ceremony, and whisked her away. So now Gary was just looking a bit blank, as if he was trying to pretend that the whole thing had never happened.

Etta, meanwhile, was backstage, as she was the star of the show. But it seemed to be taking a little while to get to that bit.

'I-i-i-t's . . . Christmas Eve!' said Bry, to another huge cheer. 'Which means it's definitely . . . *the most wonderful time of the year*!'

'TM,' said Raisa, who was standing to his right.

'Although tonight might be a good time – I think

it is – to announce that we at Winterzone are developing a new idea, which is: the most wonderful time of the year, more times in the year!'

This got less of a cheer. Well, it got a cheer, followed by a lot of voices asking, 'What?' 'Eh?' 'How does that work?'

'Yes!' continued Bry. 'Why should we only have that wonderfulness once a year! So let me take this moment to say that, from next year, Christmas – Winterzone's Christmas! – will be happening THREE times a year!'

Suddenly, there was the sound of a piano and some sleigh bells, and the gospel choir sang:

'It's Christmas, yes, it is!
Happens once a year –
But what if it happened two more times?
Well, wouldn't that make you cheer?!'

It was a short song, more of a jingle really. Afterwards there was a short pause.

'When?' shouted a voice from the crowd. It was Monty again.

Bry looked at Raisa. She shrugged. 'Um . . . well,' said Bry, 'we haven't quite worked out the details. But . . . May? And maybe . . . I dunno . . . October?'

'That's too close to the first Christmas!' shouted someone else.

'OK – September! Don't sweat the small stuff!' said Bry.

'But the whole point of Christmas is it's special!' came another voice from the crowd. 'It won't be special any more if it's three times a year!'

'OK,' said Bry. 'I get that. Thank you. All thoughts appreciated. Do text or message them to Winterzone Ideas portal.'

'At which point they become *our* ideas,' said Raisa.

'Hmm,' said Bry. 'But the point is: three times a year means THREE TIMES AS MANY PRESENTS!'

'It's Christmas, yes, it is!'

sang the gospel choir, cutting in suddenly,

'So it's gifts for you and me –
But if it happened two more times
Those gifts would be times three!!'

The song ended, and now there *was* another huge cheer. Such a huge cheer, in fact, that it drowned out Gary saying quietly: 'And three times as much money for Winterzone, of course.'

'Thank you!' said Bry to the crowd. 'I *knew* you'd like it! And speaking of presents . . . let's get right on to the main event. The big deal. The thing that is the thing. By which I mean – yes! – it's time for Perfect

Present Please! And please, to say it again, would you give it up for this year's PPP girl – it's ETTA!'

The gospel choir sang:

'It's Christmas, yes, it is!
Snowflakes on the freeze,
But we're all lovely and warm in here –
It's Perfect Present Please!!'

Everyone applauded. All the Baxters, and Monty, cheered. Jonas shouted, 'Etta is my sister!' very loudly. And Etta, led by Raisa, walked on to the stage.

CHAPTER 24

Perfect Present Please

Etta looked a little nervous when she came onstage. This was because she *was* a bit nervous. Partly because she wasn't used to being in front of an audience, but also because she wasn't sure how all this was going to turn out. Nonetheless, she waved at the audience and smiled. She too had been fitted with a head-mic. Cameras whirred and clicked. The applause died down. Raisa nudged Etta forward to stand next to Bry.

'Etta!' he said. 'Lovely to meet you!'

'Lovely to meet you too . . .'

'Bry!' said Bry. 'Call me Bry!'

'Short for . . .?'

'Never mind!' He turned to the audience. 'Now, I wanna say something about Etta. I hope this is OK for you, E.'

'That's fine, Bry.'

Gary frowned. 'That's a bit odd,' he whispered to Bonny. 'She normally only lets me and you call her that.'

'So . . . one of the things about E,' continued Bry, 'is that she . . . well, she wasn't that wild about Christmas. In the past. She was a bit of a . . . can I say this? . . . a bit of a grinch! A Scrooge!'

Etta smiled. Gary and Bonny looked at each other.

'That's not fair,' whispered Bonny. 'She loves Christmas . . . just not—'

'Winterzone's Christmas!' Gary whispered back.

'I know. Obviously I know. She's told me enough times.'

'So why is she not saying anything? That's really not like Etta!'

'Shh . . .!'

They looked round. It was Monty. He was whispering '*Shh!*' to them. 'It's OK. Just let her . . . she knows what she's doing.' He looked back to the stage. 'I think.'

'You hated Christmas, didn't you, Etta!' Bry was saying.

'Well . . .' said Etta, still smiling.

'But now,' said Bry, not waiting for a detailed response, 'you've changed your mind! You've changed your mind so much that you are . . . the Perfect Present Please girl!'

'*It's Christmas, yes, it is!*'

sang the gospel choir,

'She hated it before!

But now she's getting the perfect gift

She loves it more and more!!'

'Makes her sound a little . . . shallow,' whispered Gary.

'It'll be OK!' whispered Monty.

'Are you sure?' whispered Bonny.

'No,' whispered Monty.

'So!' said Bry. 'The time . . . has come. Etta. E. Tell us what you would like for your Perfect Present Please!'

Etta nodded. She turned to the crowd. She smiled.

'Ahem . . .' she said.

The crowd looked back at her.

'I would like . . . my perfect present . . . from Winterzone . . . to be . . .'

Etta paused. She looked round at Raisa. Etta pointed.

'. . . That orange bag there.'

CHAPTER 25

It's in the contract

'Pardon?' said Bry.

'That orange bag. The one that lady is carrying.' She pointed more closely to it. Raisa looked daggers at her. The fingers of the hand that always rested on the bag curled round it, clutching it more tightly. 'The one with the green clasps,' said Etta.

Bry looked to Raisa. Quietly, although everyone could still hear it, he said: 'I thought – you *said* – she was going to say—'

'A sparkly little collar,'

sang the gospel choir,

'For a tiny cat!
That's her Perfect Present Please,
And—'

'YES, THAT!' said Bry, cutting off the gospel choir, who looked a bit confused. *That* . . . is what we were prepared for! It's waiting for you all wrapped up!'

'That's what you told me!' said Raisa, staring at Etta.

'Yes, but I've changed my mind. I'd like that bag now. Please.'

'What about your kitten?' said Bry. 'Wee-Wee?'

'Weech,' said Etta. 'He hates wearing a collar anyway.'

'He does,' said Bonny, in the audience. 'He goes weeech weeeech weeech until we take it off!'

Bry looked at Raisa, then back at Etta. 'OK, OK. We can do this. We can get a version of that bag to you. Easy. No problem. I'll get our high-speed delivery people on to it and—'

'No,' said Etta. 'I don't want a version of that bag. I want THAT BAG. That one that she is holding.'

There was a pause. Raisa stared at her. 'Well, that's impossible,' she said. 'It's my bag. Plus it never leaves my side.'

'Well . . .' said Etta, 'I'm afraid that is what I want. And I believe that the Perfect Present Please contract I've signed . . . Is my lawyer present?'

A figure dressed in green overalls emerged from the crowd and climbed onstage. He was waving a piece of paper.

'Hello!' he said. 'I've got a copy of it here!'

'Thank you, Mr Evergreen,' said Etta.

'That guy,' whispered Bry to Raisa, ' . . . do we know him? I feel we do.'

'We do,' hissed Raisa.

'So,' said Bushy, holding the piece of paper in front of him. 'It states very clearly here in this contract signed between Etta Baxter, henceforth to be known as Etta Baxter, and Winterzone, henceforth to be known as Winterzone . . . never quite sure why these documents need to say that stuff . . . anyway, it states that . . . ahem –' here he took a pair of very old-looking glasses out of the chest pocket of his overalls and put them on his quite long nose – 'that Etta Baxter, henceforth to be blah blah, shall, on the aforementioned date, that being the twenty-fourth of December, ask for her Perfect Present Please—'

'TM,' said Raisa.

'I was going to say that,' said Bushy, looking up. 'It's in the contract.' He looked down again, re-perching his glasses. 'And . . . that her Perfect Present . . . and here's the important point—'

'Is that in the contract?' said Etta.

'No, I'm saying that.'

'Oh, right.'

'That her Perfect Present . . . whatever it might be, and notwithstanding howsoever and in whatever manner verbal or non-verbal the said Etta Baxter describes it . . . that that Present shall be brought to her immediately.'

He looked up. 'There's some small print, that goes on for seventy-four pages, but I feel it might bore your worldwide audience for me to read out all that.'

Bry looked at Bushy. He looked at Etta. He looked at the audience, watching eagerly. He looked into one of the many cameras. And then, finally, he looked at Raisa and said:

'Just give it to her.'

'What?' said Raisa.

'You heard me.'

Raisa went up to him. 'We can't do that.'

'We can. Look, just do it. We'll . . . sort it.'

Raisa took the bag off her shoulder. She held it up in front of her. Her face, which was pretty hard anyway, hardened.

'There is just no way I am letting this bag out of my—'

'Thanks!' said Etta, jumping up, grabbing the bag and running off stage.

'Perfect Present Please!

She's pleased with what she owns!

Her perfect present needs

Are met by Winterzone!!'

sang the gospel choir.

'YES! HA-HA!' said Bry, much too loudly. 'AND THAT CONCLUDES THIS YEAR'S CHRISTMAS PERFECT PRESENT PLEASE! GOODNIGHT, AND OF COURSE: HAPPY CHRISTMAS!'

Raisa took out her remote, switching off all of the many cameras trained on the stage. The audience in the Snowy Space applauded but seemed a bit confused.

Bry took off his head-mic and said to no one in particular, but maybe to everyone, or, at least, everyone at Winterzone:

'GET HER!'

CHAPTER 26

Clunk!
Doing!
Whirr!

'Where are we going?' shouted Etta, running down a corridor somewhere in the Winterzone building, Raisa's orange bag strung across her shoulder.

'I don't know!' said Monty, next to her. 'We didn't work out this bit of the plan!'

'How could we not have done that?'

'We're kids!'

'Yes, you're right. Bushy! Why didn't *you* think of it!'

Bushy, who was running behind her and very out of breath, said: 'I'm sort of a kid as well. I'm an elf. We're kind of . . . Santa's kids.'

'Right,' said Etta, who didn't much relish the idea of continuing that conversation right now. 'Meanwhile – what are we going to do!?'

'Oh! There's an exit sign here!' said Monty.

'Great!' said Etta, running towards it.

'It does worry me a little bit though,' said Monty, running with her.

'What does?' Etta was facing forward. She could see the exit doors – large glass ones – facing an enormous courtyard. They were only a few metres away.

'The fact that this is a building with cameras and computers everywhere and yet they are just going to let us run away, when Bry did just say that "Get her!" thing?'

'OK . . .' said Etta, 'but maybe . . . I dunno . . . maybe luck is on our side!'

'Maybe!' said Monty.

They were at the doors! Perhaps it was true – maybe luck WAS on their side!

Etta reached out for the handle of the biggest one—

. . . Only for a large steel shutter to come crashing down in front of her. CLUNK! DOING! WHIRR! And then the same on every door – CLUNK! DOING! WHIRR!!

They stopped, breathless.

'Or maybe not,' said a sinister, kindly, smiling voice from behind them.

CHAPTER 27

The Winterzone window

Etta and Monty and Bushy turned round. Standing facing them were Bry, Raisa, Hamnet, Hamnet and Fester.

'There's no way out of the building now, I'm afraid,' said Bry. 'Everything is shuttered. Well, there's a window up there, of course . . .'

He pointed. Way up high, past many different floors and offices, there it was: the Winterzone window, with its snow and sleigh and Santavatars dancing around the word WINTERZONE™. Etta had never seen it from the inside, with the letters the wrong way round. It threw a red and green light across the ceiling.

'Obviously we can't shutter that window as we want everyone outside to see our logo *at all times*. But, hey – I don't think any of you will be going up there any time soon and smashing through that. Will you?'

'Maybe not,' said Etta. 'But the thing is, Bry . . . I asked for my Perfect Present. This bag. And I got it. What is your problem?'

'Yeah,' said Bry. 'Good point. Here's the thing. Which is the thing. Which is. Gotta have that bag back. That's just how it is, Etta.'

'THAT'S HOW IT IS, ETTA!' screeched Hamnet. Weirdly, not the cockatoo.

'I don't think you want the world to know that Winterzone doesn't keep its promises,' said Monty boldly. 'I might make that known. I might put it on the internet!'

'Hey,' said Bry. 'That's bold.'

'I know,' said Monty.

'But, sorry, I think maybe I checked your online profile, @MontyC2010. And it didn't take us that long to count your followers on all platforms. There were . . .?'

'Seven,' said Raisa.

'Seven. Right. So, @MontyC2010, you write a *lo-o-o-o-ng-ng* thread, saying whatever you like about what's transpired here this evening and how terrible – how not OK – it makes Winterzone look. And let's see if we get cancelled, shall we?'

Monty frowned and looked down, defeated. Suddenly, Fester came out from the group. She opened a tiny bottle marked **LIFESHOT**, took a swig of it, and did a big 'AAAAAH'.

'Listen, Etta,' said Fester. 'You're a girl. I'm a girl.'

'Yes,' said Etta. 'But how old *are* you?'

'Never mind. My point is: we girls – we understand that a girl can get very . . . possessive about her bags. Right? And so Raisa – she just needs her bag back.' Fester smiled and scrunched up her nose in a way that Etta understood was meant to be adorable. But it just made her face look very strange. 'Because she's such a *girl*!'

Etta looked over at Raisa. Raisa was looking at her blankly. She put her hand out blankly.

'I don't think so,' said Etta, shaking her head. 'I think you must really want this bag because there's something inside it that's very, VERY important.'

'Well,' said Bry, 'if that's what you think . . . open the bag.'

'Pardon?'

'Open the bag, Etta. No probs. Go ahead. If that's your thing, that is your thing. Totes opes.'

Etta looked down. She had been clutching the

bag close to her without realising it. Carefully, she moved it away from her waist an inch and put her fingers to the green clasps at the top of it. They didn't move.

She looked up. Raisa was holding up her tiny remote.

'It's locked,' she said simply.

'You can lock a bag with a remote?' said Monty.

'You'd better believe it, Monty,' said Bry. 'Tech-knowledgey. Remember?'

'Yes. Although I still can't work out how you're spelling that.'

'T-E-C— Oh, we don't have time for this. You've lost.'

'I thought there were no winners and losers in Winterzone?' said Etta.

'Ha ha, yeah,' said Bry. 'No, you've definitely lost. Hand over the bag.'

Etta looked at Monty and Bushy Evergreen. If she

couldn't open it, there didn't seem much point in holding on to it. But something made her say: 'No. Sorry. It's my Perfect Present Please.'

Bry nodded. 'OK. I get that. I hear what you're saying.' He continued to nod. 'But I think we're in a different space to you on that. CWX25?'

'Mark 2' said a smooth voice. The robot appeared from behind him.

'Go get the bag,' said Bry.

CHAPTER 28

No problemo

'No problemo,' said CWX25.

'Don't say that,' said Bry.

'No problemo,' said CWX25.

'You've said it again.'

'Yes,' said the robot. 'I meant it was no problem to stop saying "no problemo". Unfortunately, I am now caught in a loop of saying "no problemo".'

'JUST GO AND GET THE BAG, CWX25 MARK 2.'

'No problemo,' said the robot. Bry bit his tongue

to stop himself from telling the robot not to say it again. CWX25 Mark 2's head whirred towards Etta. He started towards her.

'Give me the bag, Etta,' he said.

'No!'

'Give me the bag, Etta.'

'I can't do that, CWX25 Mark 2.'

'Well, you can,' said the robot, and reached out a hand. He was close to her now. Etta could hear a small whirring sound coming from his body. She tried to swerve away, but the robot's hand suddenly moved towards the bag at an incredible speed. She felt the strength of his fingers pulling at the bag. Etta shut her eyes, clutching it as tightly as she could, but she knew she wouldn't be able to hold on.

And then, suddenly, there was a huge whooshing sound, and a large crash, and she felt the pressure of the robot's fingers on the bag go. She opened her eyes.

'ETTA! BUSHY! MONTY! QUICKLY! GET IN!'

Etta blinked. It was quite hard to work out what was happening. It was her dad who was shouting. But it wasn't at first clear where he was shouting *from*.

It also wasn't clear why CWX25 Mark 2 had ended up on the ground, with a dent in his head. Or why Bry, Hamnet, Fester and Raisa were all ducking down, looking frightened. Or why Hamnet the cockatoo was flying around frantically in circles, screeching 'HAMNET? HAMNET? IS IT A BIG BIRD? THAT WILL EAT ME?!'

But then she looked up and saw that
her dad – and, seated behind him, her mum
and Jonas too – were hovering about a metre above
her, in what looked like an amazing, sleek, futuristic
red-and-white spaceship.

'What is THAT?' she said.

'It's the Super-Sleigh, of course!' shouted her dad, bringing it down to her level. 'NOW GET IN!'

CHAPTER 29

The Super-Sleigh

She reached out her arms, and her dad pulled her into the sleigh to sit next to him. As she did so, Monty and Bushy Evergreen clambered in round the back to join Bonny and Jonas.

'OMG, Dad!' said Etta, looking at the range of dials and lights in front of her. Her dad was holding on to the steering wheel. 'It's amazing!'

'Thanks!' said Gary proudly. He pulled back on the steering wheel. The Super-Sleigh hovered up another couple of metres. 'I was only able to get to it and fly it here because they called the robot away to come and deal with you! Oh, it felt good to knock him over just now!'

'Um . . . Mr Baxter,' said Monty. 'I think maybe CWX25 and the others haven't quite been vanquished yet . . .'

Etta and Gary looked down. Bry and the other Winterzoners had got up and were staring up in some amazement at the Super-Sleigh. But CWX25 Mark 2, despite the dent in his head, was rising off the floor and flying towards them.

'Wow!' said Etta. 'I didn't know he had jet-pack feet!'

'Neither did I!' said Gary.

'Oh yes!' shouted Hamnet the non-cockatoo from below them.

'OH YES!' screeched Hamnet the cockatoo from above them.

CWX25 Mark 2 was now hovering in front of the sleigh. He said, in his smooth voice (but with a tinny rasp now, possibly because the dent did go across his mouth), 'Please bring the Super-Sleigh down to the ground, Gary.'

'Oh, not this again.'

'Gary. Please bring the Super-Sleigh down.'

'Shut up, CWX25 Mark 2!'

'Santa! Santa! Santa!' said Jonas.

'That's not Santa!' said Etta.

'Not the real Santa?' he said, sounding sad.

'No! Every time you say "Santa!" it's *never* Santa. You see Santa everywhere. But it isn't him. It's a Santavatar or a cartoon . . . and this time it's a robot in a Christmas jumper.'

'Oh, don't make him cry, Etta!' said Bonny. And Etta did feel a bit bad about having said it.

'Guys – I really think we've got other things to worry about' said Bushy Evergreen, as CWX25 Mark 2 started moving in the air towards them, arms outstretched.

'Unless you bring the Super-Sleigh down to the ground, Gary, I will clamp myself on to it and bring you down to the ground by switching my jet-pack feet to reverse,' he said calmly. He was floating about two metres away . . . and closing.

'That's interesting – they actually *are* called jet-pack feet,' said Monty to Etta. 'I thought you'd just made that up on the spot . . .'

'Dad!' said Etta. 'Quickly! Let's get out of here!'

'But . . . there's nowhere to go!' said Gary. 'They've closed the shutters!'

'WE HAVE!' said Bry. 'SO YOU MIGHT AS WELL COME DOWN ANYWAY!' He lowered his voice and smiled, looking round at Hamnet, Hamnet, Fester and Raisa. 'If you want to, of course. I never give anyone who works at Winterzone a direct order. You know me – I just hate that whole boss-employee power dynamic.' He looked back at Gary. 'BUT I WOULD IF I WERE YOU, BAXTER!'

'DAD!' shouted Etta. 'Let's go!'

'Where?' he replied weakly.

Whirr, whirr, went CWX25 Mark 2's arms as they moved like a crab's pincers towards the front of the Super-Sleigh.

'UP THERE!' shouted Etta. 'THROUGH THE WINTERZONE WINDOW!'

Her dad looked up. He gasped. 'The *Winterzone window*! I can't break the Winterzone window . . .'

'YOU CAN, DAD!'

'I can't!'

'Mr Baxter,' said Monty, leaning over. 'Look . . . this company has ground you down. It's ignored you and your brilliant work on this sleigh for years! It seems to me that you don't owe them anything at—'

THUMP!

'The robot's clamped on!' said Bonny.

'Oh,' said Monty. 'Perhaps we don't have time to discuss it at length.'

'I am sorry about this, Gary,' said CWX25 Mark 2. His eyes flashed and whirred, and jet flames roared from his feet. 'GOING DOWN . . .' the robot said.

CHAPTER 30

Powersurge

The force of the robot jets began pulling them down to the ground, where Bry, Hamnet, cockatoo Hamnet (who had now landed on human Hamnet's shoulder), Fester and Raisa were waiting. Bry was smiling. He had opened his arms towards them.

'Dad!' shouted Etta. 'Do something!'

Gary was holding on to the steering wheel of the Super-Sleigh. His face was white. He shook his head.

'Not sure there's anything he can do, E!' said Bry, speaking up to them. 'And hey, Gary – I have to say that is a smart-looking machine you've made here. You've done well. I think . . . you know what? . . . I think it's going to look *really* good in photoshoots and memes. We might even do a corporate video of it. What do you say?'

Gary looked over. For the first time, Etta saw her father's face change into something angry and strong.

'I say . . .' he said, 'you and Winterzone can go to hell!'

And with that, he leaned back and pulled hard on the steering wheel, like an aeroplane joystick. Immediately, the Super-Sleigh roared like a huge mechanical lion. The back of it shot up, while the front was still being held, and pushed down, by CWX25 Mark 2.

'AAARGGGH!' shouted Bushy, falling forward.

'Santa! Stop it! Go away!' shouted Jonas.

'He's not Santa!' shouted Etta.

Gary pressed a button on the dashboard marked POWERSURGE.

'HOLD ON!' he shouted.

The Super-Sleigh roared again. Its roar started to overcome the (also pretty roaring) sound of CWX25's jet-pack feet.

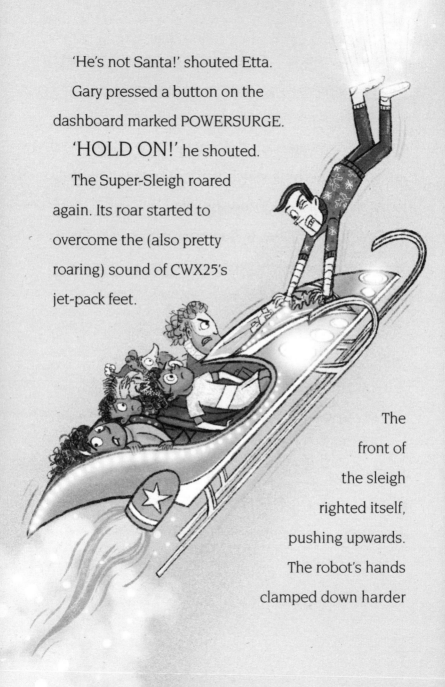

The front of the sleigh righted itself, pushing upwards. The robot's hands clamped down harder on the front. But it made no difference. The Super-Sleigh was definitely moving slowly upwards. The robot looked up at the Baxters and Monty and Bushy Evergreen sitting in the Super-Sleigh. Then his face did something which had not seemed entirely possible before: it looked confused.

Seeing that, Gary pulled back harder again on the steering wheel. The sleigh's engine roared even more. It jerked upwards, throwing CWX25 Mark 2 off its nose. He tumbled, somersaulting, towards the ground. BANG! That's him hitting the ground.

'CWX25 Mark 2!' cried human Hamnet, as if he'd seen his child hit by a car.

'CWX . . . Can't remember the numbers! Can't remember the numbers!' screeched Hamnet the cockatoo.

'Its . . . the . . . most . . . wonderful . . . time . . . of . . . the . . . .yeaaaaaaaa . . .' sang CWX25 very, very slowly, face up on the ground. He sounded even worse than Mark 1 had.

The Super-Sleigh, free of robot weight, surged upwards. It hovered just below the ceiling. Just in front of the long Winterzone window.

'Don't do this, Baxter,' shouted Bry. 'You're a Winterzone man. I know you are.'

Monty leaned over again from the back seat. 'As I said before, Gary – they've ground you into the dust; they've ignored you and your brilliant work for years. They—'

'Yes, all right, Monty,' said Gary, without looking round. 'DUCK DOWN, EVERYONE!' He pushed the steering wheel forward, and the sleigh flew at high speed towards the long Winterzone window.

CHAPTER 31

Hold on!

SMASH!

Through the window the Super-Sleigh went! But it didn't just smash it in one go. The glass cracked at one corner, where there was a row of olde-worlde houses with snow on their rooftops, and Gary had to rev the engine once more and reverse and come back and smash into the window again!

'AAAARGGGH!' went everyone in the Super-Sleigh.

They hit it square in the middle, right in the centre, between the E and the R. The whole thing shattered in one go. Through her eyes covered with her hands, Etta could see the letters W and N and Z and all the others – and the Santavatars and the snowflakes and the cartoon sleighs – disintegrate and fall away.

'AAAARGGGH!' screamed everybody in the Super-Sleigh, as they went through the window and out into the night air. The noise of the shattering glass echoed behind them. The sleigh swung about in the air with the force of the blow. Gary threw the steering wheel one way and the other, trying to get it under control. It dipped and dived. It was windy up in the air outside the building, and cold.

'HOLD ON!' said Gary.

Even through her fear – and

feeling not a little bit sick – Etta found herself impressed, thinking that maybe, underneath it all, her dad wasn't such a wimp after all.

The sleigh finally steadied. Which allowed Etta to look over the side. The sun was setting, and the city lights underneath were starting to come on. As they moved further and further away from Winterzone, all the noise – of the window breaking, of the roaring of the sleigh through it, of the shouting of Bry and the rest of his people – eventually died down. Etta looked over at her dad. He was looking out, but he seemed to sense that her eyes were on him and he turned round.

'Are you OK?' he said.

'Fine, Dad. That was amazing. *This* is amazing. I'm so *proud* of you!'

He blushed and smiled. 'Thanks. To be honest, I wasn't sure until just now that it could actually fly. I mean, I built it to, even though – as Bry kept on saying – it didn't need to. But it was important to me that it could. And that I knew how to fly it. And turns out . . . it does, and I can!'

He flicked a switch in front of him. The sleigh settled into an easy cruising speed.

'Yes, I'm proud of you too!' said Bonny. 'But just one thing. Where are we going now?'

Gary frowned. 'Hmm. That is a good question. Home, I guess.' He looked out over the city, towards where he thought their flat might be. 'I don't know if I can land this in the road outside our flat though.'

'We might have to upgrade the parking permit,' said Bonny.

'But we're only allowed one vehicle per household,' he replied.

'Hmm, good point,' she replied.

'Mum . . .' said Etta. 'I don't think we can go to our flat yet. Because – sorry to break it to you, but – the whole point of me doing Perfect Present Please,

and asking for this instead of a collar for Weech –'
she indicated Raisa's bag, still strapped across her
shoulder – 'was because . . . well, we – me, Monty
and Bushy – we think in here is . . .' And her face
went a little red at this point, because she knew it
sounded silly. '. . . Is Santa Claus's – the *real* Santa
Claus's – contract. With Winterzone.'

Gary looked at her. He put the sleigh into hover
mode. It stopped in the sky.

'Sorry, can you run that past me again?' he said
eventually.

CHAPTER 32

Credelftials

Some minutes later, Etta (with some help from Bushy and Monty) had explained everything: about going to see the XMX delivery guy in the donkey sanctuary in the forest, about him admitting that he was Santa, and about the contract he had signed with Winterzone.

'And that's why we need to go and see him!' She held up the bag. 'To tear up this thing and let him be Santa again!'

'Right . . .' said Gary, a bit doubtfully.

'More than that, in fact,' Etta continued. 'To make Christmas *real* again.' She looked round at Monty and Bushy. 'That was our plan! Mine and Monty and Bushy's plan!'

Bonny leaned over from the back of the sleigh.

'Why is that so important to you, darling?' she said.

Etta looked at her. Her voice cracked a little, and she wiped her eyes. Maybe because they were so

high up. Maybe. 'Because . . . because of Grandma
Jo . . .'

Gary looked at her. He didn't speak. He let her
continue.

'Because I remember what she told me. About
how there used to be another version of Christmas.
A better version. And maybe somewhere there still
is.'

'Etta . . .' said Gary. 'That's lovely. It really is.
But . . . I hate to break this to you —' he looked

round – 'to all of you. But I don't think . . . I really don't know if I believe that this . . . *delivery guy* who lives in the forest *is* the real Santa.'

'Oh, he is,' said Bushy Evergreen. 'Or I am not a real elf.'

'Right. Well, you see, I'm not absolutely sure about that, either.'

Bushy went very red indeed. 'How very dare you,' he said. 'Do I need to show you my credelftials?'

'Your what?' said Bonny.

'My credelftials.'

'You see, it's that kind of pun that makes me think perhaps I shouldn't take you entirely seriously,' said Gary.

Bushy shook his head, and with a disappointed voice replied: 'Clearly you haven't been paying much attention to Christmas crackers. I write a fair few of those every year!'

'Look, Etta,' said Gary. 'Let's just go home. We

can talk about this tomorrow.'

'But tomorrow is Christmas Day, Dad!'

'OK. Well, after Christmas then. What's the hurry?'

BEEP. BEEP. A sound came from somewhere. Everyone looked over, worried that it might be a beep indicating something wrong with the sleigh. But it was just Gary's phone.

He picked it up and looked worried. Very worried.

'What is it?' said Etta.

He turned round. 'It's a message. A press release in fact. From Bryan Leaf, on behalf of Winterzone.'

Etta frowned. 'Saying what?'

'Saying that, due to a break-in at Winterzone . . . the computers have been *sabotaged* . . . by terrible evil people!'

'They haven't been!' said Etta. 'What are they talking about?'

'And because of that . . . they are shutting down all operations. All deliveries. The presents . . . will be staying in the Winterzone warehouse until further notice.'

There was a silence. Around them, the wind whistled.

'What does that mean?' said Etta eventually, her throat dry – and not just because she was high up in the atmosphere.

'It means . . .' Gary said, and his voice sounded strangled, '. . . that, um, basically . . . out of revenge . . . Winterzone are cancelling Christmas! For everyone!' He looked at her. 'And they're making it *our* fault!' He shook his head.

'That's terrible!' said Monty.

'Yes!' said Gary.

Another silence. Then Gary said: 'So . . . what are we going to do?!'

Everyone on the Super-Sleigh went very quiet. Except for Jonas, who said plaintively:

'Santa! Santa! Santa?'

Etta blinked. Her face changed. 'Good idea, Jonas. Dad, we've got no choice now. So please can you go . . .?' She turned round towards Bushy.

Bushy, understanding immediately, stood up and pointed in the distance, towards what looked like, in the golden light of the sun going down, a green forest.

'That way,' he said.

PART FOUR:

DO I *REALLY* NEED TO SAY IT AGAIN?

CHAPTER 33

Good luck with that

'AAARRGGGHHH!!! GET OUT OF HERE!
GO AWAY!! BEFORE I CALL THE POLICE!'

Said Santa.

Things were not going that well for Etta, Monty
and Bushy. It was getting late. They had flown above
the forest and found exactly the place they needed
to be, but when they came down to land, the wind
around the sleigh had knocked over the splintered
and broken wooden fence, and the splintered and

broken wooden house – well, more of a shed really. All that was left were some planks and the 'BRACKET WOOD DONKEY SANCTUARY' sign. And even that was split in half.

The XMX delivery guy, as far as Bonny and Gary were concerned, or Santa, as far as Etta, Monty and Bushy were concerned . . . let's just call him Santa, was standing in front of the field of donkeys and one reindeer. The donkeys and one reindeer had watched complacently as the Super-Sleigh landed. But Santa was shouting very loudly and waving his arms about.

'YOU'VE DESTROYED THE DONKEY SANCTUARY!'

'Sorry!' said Etta, getting out of the sleigh.

'Well, we haven't really,' said Monty, also getting out. 'We've just destroyed the splintered and broken wooden house – well, more of a shed really – in front of it. The *donkeys* and reindeer look fine.'

'He does have a point there, Claus,' said Bushy.

'NO, HE DOESN'T, EVERGREEN!'

'Um . . .' whispered Bonny, still sitting in the sleigh, to Gary, who was still sitting there too. 'Do you think that maybe he actually *is* . . .'

'Oh, don't be silly, darling,' said Gary, looking round. Bonny was holding Jonas, who was staring very hard at the shouting man.

'WHAT DO YOU WANT!?' yelled Santa.

'Do you know what's happened?' said Etta.

'YOU'VE DESTROYED MY DONKEY AND ONE REINDEER SANCTUARY, THAT'S WHAT'S HAPPENED!'

'I think we've been over this,' said Monty. 'Meanwhile, can everyone turn their phones off!'

'Why?' said Gary.

'Because otherwise Winterzone will be able to track us. They will know where we are!'

Gary shrugged but took out his phone and did so, along with the others.

'And talking of Winterzone,' said Etta, '*that's* what's

happened. They've cancelled Christmas!'

Santa stared at her. 'What?' he said, finally lowering his voice.

'They have. They did it because . . . because we went in there – to Winterzone – to get something . . . something to help you . . .'

'We stole something really. Technically,' said Bushy.

'Is that necessary to say?' said Etta.

He shrugged. 'I'm a lawyer.'

'Stole what?' said Santa.

'This,' said Etta. She took Raisa's orange bag off her shoulder. Santa looked at it. He frowned.

'Is that . . .?'

'It's Raisa's bag. Where Bushy thinks your contract is kept.'

Santa took a deep breath. 'Yes. I know that's what he thinks. Is it?'

'Well . . .' said Etta, trying again, her small fingers

doing their best to prise apart the green clasps at the top. 'We can't open it.'

'I'm sorry, can I interrupt?' said Gary, appearing suddenly. 'Hello there. I think you came to our flat a while back, didn't you? To deliver something. Or not. Anyway. I think we may need to be going soon. I'm not sure any of this really makes sense.'

Santa eyed him suspiciously. 'Any of what?'

'Any of this . . . weird story. About you being . . . y'know . . . him.'

'Him?'

'You know,' said Monty. 'Saint Nicholas. Kris Kringle. Papa Noël. Baba Chaghaloo. Hotei-Osho.'

'Bless you,' said Gary.

'No, it's the name of a Buddhist monk who in Japan is the equivalent of—'

'Well,' said Santa, coming up close to Gary, 'if you really want to know, sir, I can tell you that I definitely *am*—'

'No,' said Bushy firmly. 'Remember the NDA.'

'Eh?'

'ND. And then, indeed, A. You can't tell him anything.'

Santa looked exasperated. He pointed to Etta and Monty. 'But I've already told *them*!'

'Yes, but they're kids. And traditionally, in stories, particularly stories where kids get wind of magic stuff happening before anyone else, adults don't believe them. I think, legally, that makes it OK.'

'Have you been drinking?' said Gary.

'No. As I said, I'm a lawyer,' said Bushy.

'Not you. Him.'

'Just a tiny smidge of sherry,' said Santa defensively. 'To get me through the cold winter nights.'

'OK. Etta! Monty!' said Gary. 'Let's go!'

'No!' said Etta, trying once again to force the

clasps. Her face grew pained with the effort. 'We have to open this bag!'

Bonny came over. She put her arm round Etta. 'Etta, darling. It's getting late. And it's Christmas Day tomorrow.'

'Well, it's not,' said Etta, starting to sound tearful. 'Because of what Winterzone have done!'

'Maybe . . .' said Bonny, looking up. She was holding Jonas, who was still staring at Santa. She addressed everyone. 'Maybe the lesson here is that . . . we don't *need* presents. For Christmas. Maybe Christmas isn't all about presents. It's about something else. Isn't it? Family. And tradition. And love. About spending time together.' As she spoke, her eyes went up towards the sky. It was almost like you could hear music swelling beneath her as she spoke. 'We can make it special – we can still make it the most wonderful time of the year – without presents. Can't we?'

'Yeah,' said Monty, grabbing the bag off Etta and gripping the clasps with his fingers as hard as he could. 'Good luck with that.'

CHAPTER 34

Prancer

But Monty couldn't open the bag either. Gary came over and looked more closely at it.

'Yes . . . I'd say that's got a 58XJG on it.'

'What's that?' said Monty, puffing.

'It's a Winterzone-generated digital lock. It can only be opened with an encoded laser key.'

'Oh . . .' said Monty, giving up. 'Have you got one of those?'

'No. They are made at TinselTech 2. I'm TinselTech 1.'

'Yes. I know that.'

'So again, I'd say . . . y'know – it was a lovely plan, but maybe, guys . . .'

'Oh, for heaven's sake,' said Santa. 'Prancer!'

'Pardon?' said Gary.

'PRANCER!'

Everyone looked round. Slowly – and without having to worry about getting over the fence, because that had been blown down – the fragile-looking reindeer wandered over to them. His antlers, this close up, looked a bit scratched and worse for wear. His big brown eyes looked up at Santa.

'You may not fancy this for your tea,' said Santa, 'but as we know . . . you're hungry. Because –' he looked at Bushy – 'there aren't any carrots!' He looked down at the bag. 'And at least this bag looks a bit like one.'

'Wha—' said Etta. But before she could continue, Santa had grabbed the bag from Monty's hands and was holding it in front of Prancer's nose.

Prancer looked at it: the orange bag with the green clasps. His eyes widened. And suddenly he opened his massive jaw and chomped down on the top of it.

'Thanking you!' said Santa, pulling the rest of the bag out of the reindeer's mouth. 'I knew those enormous teeth were still working!'

He held up the torn remains of the bag. Prancer munched. He seemed fairly happy with the meal. He burped.

'Claus!' cried Bushy. 'Can you make sure he hasn't *eaten* the contract! I don't think – if we want to make it null and void – that I can swing that in court. "My reindeer ate it"? No. It sounds rubbish. Like saying "my dog ate it" when a teacher asks for your homework.'

'Calm down, Evergreen,' said Santa, putting the large gnarled fingers of his right hand into the bottom half of the orange bag – well, it wasn't really a bag any more, more a piece of cloth with a long serrated edge – and fumbling around. 'Let's see if your instinct was right! Aha!'

He pulled his hand out. And with it came a rolled-up piece of paper, with a small red ribbon tied in a bow round it. He took the ribbon off and unrolled the paper.

'YES! Here it is . . .' He passed it to Bushy. 'Do your lawyer thang, then . . .'

Bushy held it open, like an old-fashioned town crier. 'Ahem. Yes. It says . . . "I, Santa Claus, otherwise known as Father Christmas, Saint Nick, Sinterklaas, Deda Mraz, Chilling Grandpa, Old Man Winter, Hotei-Osho . . ."'

'Maybe don't read them all . . .' said Monty.

'Right, no . . . "I pledge, on the signing of this document, to cease to perform any Santa-like duties, to include all or part of: making lists of naughty slash nice children, riding a flying sleigh laden with presents, sliding down chimneys, delivering said presents underneath Christmas trees, and saying the word 'ho' three times . . ." Actually, that last bit's been crossed out.'

'Told you!' said Santa. 'Ho ho ho.'

'"I also . . ."' continued Bushy, '"agree not to tell anyone about this." Maybe some children who no one will believe, but definitely no adults . . .'

Santa looked at him. 'You made the last bit up, right?'

'Ho ho ho!' said Bushy.

CHAPTER 35

The spirit of Christmas

'Yes, but doesn't you reading this out – about who you are – break the NDA on this contract anyway?' said Gary.

Bushy looked up. He opened his mouth, then shut it again. 'Hmm. Might need to brush up a bit on that lawyer thang.'

'So . . .' said Etta, grabbing the contract out of Bushy's hands and going towards Santa. 'This is what we did. For you. We found it. The document that stops you being Santa. And we brought it to you.'

She held it out to him.

'So, Santa . . . you need to tear it up.'

'Um . . .' said Bushy, 'as your lawyer, I have to advise against that . . . just as I previously advised against it being eaten by Rud—'

'And then,' said Etta, ignoring him, 'you need to get in the Super-Sleigh – the one my dad designed; that amazing machine over there – and deliver all the presents to all the children who are waiting for them.' She came closer. 'You need to *be* Santa again!'

He looked at Etta. 'Right,' he said.

'N*ow*,' she said.

Santa sighed very deeply. He held out his hands and took the document from her.

'I . . . don't know, Etta.'

'Why?'

He sat down on a nearby tree stump. 'Because I

signed this for a reason.' He paused. 'Because I'm old. And tired.'

'I know. But they broke the agreement. Winterzone. They said they'd stick to the spirit of Christmas. But they didn't!'

'I know, Etta,' he said heavily. 'I know. But that doesn't . . .' He looked up. His face was drawn. His beard shone very white in the moonlight. 'That doesn't stop me being old and tired.'

There was a silence. No one knew what to say. Monty looked at Etta. She seemed to be blinking back tears.

'Maybe we should leave him be . . .' said Monty.

'No! No. Wait . . .' She ran over to the Super-Sleigh and reached inside. She came out again. She was holding her school bag.

She put it down on the ground in front of the tree stump and unzipped it. She reached inside and took out . . . an old white shoebox. She handed the box to the old man on the tree stump.

He looked at it. He looked at the writing on it.

'"Do Not Open Until . . ."'

'"The REAL . . ."'

'"The REAL Christmas".' He looked up at her. 'Is that now?'

Etta shut her eyes. 'I don't know. She opened them again. 'But it's nearer than it's been for a while.' She nodded at him to open the box. He took the lid off.

One by one he took out the things inside.

A small piece of silver tinsel. It glittered in his dark eyes.

A shiny red bauble. He held it up. Etta could see his face, his beard, his sadness reflected in it.

A gold Christmas cracker. ('Shall we pull this?' he said. 'Maybe not yet,' said Etta.)

And a little crayon drawing of Santa flying his sleigh across the moon.

'Who gave you this?' he said.

'My Grandma Jo,' said Etta. 'The last Christmas she had with us.' She turned away. 'She used to really love Christmas. The way it used to be.'

The man on the stump nodded. Carefully, with great delicacy, so as to make sure not to break anything, he put everything back in the box. He looked up.

'Please, Santa . . .' said Etta.

'I . . .' he said. 'I . . . maybe . . . but . . . I'm still not sure . . . not sure I want to . . .'

'You really don't,' said a voice. A kindly, smiley voice, sounding more sinister than ever.

CHAPTER 36
The real Santa

'**B**ry!' said Gary. 'Hamnet, Hamnet, Raisa and Fester!'

'Yes,' said Bry. 'It's us.' They were standing in a line, facing everyone. Behind them, in the clearing, stood a very large, very black electric car. 'You didn't think you'd get rid of us that easily, did you?'

'That's a bit of a panto-villain line, Bry,' said Monty. 'To be honest.'

'Oh, is it, Monty? Is it? Well. Sorry about that.

Not as sorry as the person among you who, even in this godforsaken off-grid area, left their phone on, I imagine. So that we could trace you. Who would be . . .' He looked to Raisa.

She got out her remote control and pressed a button. A screen appeared out of nowhere, just in the night air, with Monty's face on it and a whole bunch of data about him.

'Monty Cohen, of 41A Shackleton Avenue. Eleven years, three months old. Most visited sites: Infopedia, Knowledge dot com, SmartAlec dot net . . .'

'Oh dear,' said Monty, getting his phone out. 'You know when I told everyone to turn their phones off . . .?'

'You forgot to turn your own one off?' said Gary.

'Yes! How ironic.'

'But not in a funny way,' said Gary.

'I guess not,' said Monty.

'But thank you, Monty,' said Bry. 'For that. Now. sir,' he said, approaching Santa Claus, who was looking more and more just like the XMX delivery guy. 'We watched that beautiful scene. Just now. With the white shoebox. And stuff. The guys were saying: "Let's go break this up!"'

'LET'S GO BREAK THIS UP!' screeched Hamnet.

'Thank you, Hamnet,' said Bry.

'That was me, not the cockatoo,' said Hamnet.

'OK,' said Bry. 'Anyway. I said no. Let's watch. It's so amazing. The whole thing with the dead grandma . . .' He put his hand on his chest. 'Heart-warming. Really. Emotion like that: we can always use that. At Winterzone, I mean. It's what makes people *really* want to buy stuff.'

Etta grabbed the box and put it back in her school bag. She didn't like the way Bry was talking about it.

Bry was focused only on the man on the tree stump.

'But hey. Listen. Sir. Of course – it's your choice. That document. It *is* binding. Can't get round that. I think you know what happens if you renege on it. And . . .' He screwed his face up and his eyes become tiny. 'No one wants that. Do they? You certainly don't. Not with the number of children who already . . . well, not to put too fine a point on it, *don't* believe in you.' Santa looked pained, as if these words were a punch to his stomach. 'But hey,' continued Bry, 'if you want to tear it up, tear it up. It's your thing, that is the thing. Your call. As I'm sure your little lawyer elf could tell you.'

'Less of the "little",' said Bushy.

Bry was actually now sitting on the stump next to Santa. 'But just remember. All that sherry. All that *rest*. All that *time*, sir. Time to do nothing. Time you can spend relaxing – which is what you should be doing at your time of life, not having to spend all year at the beck and call of –' he put his arm round the man's shoulders and looked out, particularly at Etta and Monty – 'frankly, *spoiled* kids. Working yourself to death, so that they can – let's be honest – have their greed satisfied.' He hugged the man tight and put his face close to him. 'Let *us* do that. Let Winterzone take that burden from you. Forever. I mean . . . we've got the guys!'

Bry nodded at Raisa. She pressed a button on her remote control. Suddenly, all over the clearing, against the trees, against mounds of snow, Santavatars appeared, *loads* of them, waving and grinning and saying, 'Ho ho ho!' and 'Happy Christmas!' A few appeared to be just saying 'Winterzone!' Everyone looked at them. Fester and Hamnet clapped. Bird Hamnet clapped his wings.

'Ha!' said Bry. 'I mean: how great is this! *Hundreds* of Santas! Much better than just the one really. So, come on – what reason do you have to keep doing it. Really?'

He looked around, as if daring anyone present to answer. As he did so, he put one hand on the contract, gently tugging it away from the old man's hands.

No one said anything. Monty felt guilty. Bushy was looking at the ground. Gary and Bonny were doing that exchanging-glances thing again. And Etta felt she'd done her best, given her everything, with her box.

So no one spoke. No one except . . .

'SANTA! SANTA! SANTA!!'

'Pardon?' said Bry. 'Who was that?'

'SANTA! THE REAL SANTA! I CAN SEE THE REAL SANTA!'

It was Jonas. A three-and-a-half-year-old child, in his mother's arms. Pointing.

Etta looked over.

'SANTA!' said Jonas, pointing right at him. Etta saw the man on the stump look up. She saw him fix his gaze on Jonas.

'Ha ha!' said Bry, gesturing towards all the Santavatars. 'You mean . . . these fellows, yes? Right, little guy?'

'NO!' said Jonas, pointing again. 'JUST THAT ONE. SANTA!'

'Put him down, Mum!' cried Etta excitedly.

'Eh?' said Bonny.

'PUT HIM DOWN!'

Bonny looked at Gary. Gary looked uncertain. But he nodded.

Bonny put Jonas down.

'SANTA! THE REAL SANTA!'

'Yes!' said Etta. 'YES, JONAS. This time you are right! HE REALLY IS!'

Jonas walked towards the man on the tree stump.

He got there and said, one more time (this time more quietly):

'Santa.'

He put his arms round the old man's neck.

And Santa said:

'Yes.'

CHAPTER 37

The naughty list

Then Santa got up and pulled the contract away from Bry.

'Now. Sir. Come on,' said Bry. 'Don't do anything you might regret.'

'I won't,' Santa said. 'That would be awful.'

With that, he held out the contract. Using the tips of his fingers, he tore it in half. There was a loud tearing sound, much louder somehow than it should've been.

'Oh my days,' said Fester.

'That's torn it!' said Hamnet.

'Good one,' said bird Hamnet.

'Thanks,' said Hamnet.

'This is a *bad* thing,' said Bry. 'A really bad thing, that is the *bad thing*.'

As he spoke, something was happening, though. Santa, having got up from the tree stump, looked suddenly . . . not young, obviously, but stronger, fitter. He took off his XMX overalls.

'Bushy! Have you still got my—'

'Of course I have!' said Bushy. 'I was never going to chuck *that* out! In fact . . .'

Bushy had got it ready for him: a long red jacket lined in all the right places with white ermine fur. He stood on the tree stump and placed it round Santa's shoulders.

'SANTA!' said Jonas. 'THE SANTA!'

'Yes,' said Etta. 'Yes, yes, yes, yes, yes!!'

Bushy now gave him a pair of white gloves, which Santa fitted on to his hands. And lastly, Bushy placed on top of Santa's head a long, red hat with a white bobble.

'Bonny,' whispered Gary, 'I know this is ridiculous, but I am starting to think that maybe he IS . . . the . . .'

'Gary,' said Santa.

'Um, yes?'

'Call me Mr Claus.'

'OK.'

'How difficult is that thing –' he gestured to the Super-Sleigh – 'to ride. Out of ten?'

'Um . . . six? I tried to keep it very simple,' said Gary.

'And it's superfast?'

'It is.' Gary looked at him. 'And . . . of course . . . you're welcome to use it, Mr Claus.'

Santa smiled. He clapped his hand on Gary's shoulder. 'Thank you, Gary.' Then he came over to where Etta was standing. He crouched down. There was a knee-cracking sound, but it didn't seem to bother him. 'And thank *you*, Etta. You were right. I had forgotten who I was. And what I'm meant to do. And you . . .' He put his face close to hers. 'You reminded me.'

Etta looked at him. Then she threw her arms round him and gave him – the real Santa, whose hair and beard now seemed suddenly to be flowing and white – an enormous hug.

'Ho ho ho!' he said. He broke off the hug, turned and climbed into the sleigh. Then Bushy climbed in after him. 'PRANCER! You coming?' Santa shouted.

They all watched open-mouthed as the reindeer trotted up and, in one bound, leaped into the sleigh too.

'Isn't he meant to be at the front of it?' said Monty.

'I think it'll be fine for him to have a night off,' said Santa. 'But I still want him along for the ride. And he'll want to come – for the carrots, of course!'

'Oh, for crying out loud,' said Bry. 'You know what's going to happen now, sir? We will make it known that you – that you don't exist! That no one should believe in you!'

'OK,' said Santa. 'But you know what, Bryan?'

'Bry.'

'You know what, Bryan? I've had to live with that forever. There were always those who didn't believe.

It's up to the world – to children – whether they want to believe in me or not. Like it always is. And you can put out as much misinformation about me as you want. Fact is: kids tomorrow all over the world are going to be waking up to presents in their stockings. So. Put that in your virtual vape stick and smoke it!'

He started the engine. It made a huge lion's roar!

'But . . .' said Bry, starting to sound a bit desperate. 'But that plan is not going to work. Because all the presents are in the Winterzone warehouse.'

'Yes. I know. We'll pop there first.'

'Ha! It's shut down and locked. Digitally locked. Sir. So, hey – best of luck with *that*.'

'Wow,' said Santa. 'But you know what? I think it might be OK. What with me having *thousands of years of experience of breaking into buildings*. I don't think I've forgotten how to do that. But thanks for the heads up, Bryan.'

Bry looked at him.

'It's Bry.'

'Oh no. I remember you from when you were a kid. And you were very much on the naughty list. At the top. It was *Bryan*. So anyway . . . ready, guys? See ya!'

He flicked another switch and, with another huge roar, the Super-Sleigh hovered up from the ground. Then it powered off above the trees towards the moon, throwing a silhouette on to it, a silhouette that looked just like a little girl's crayon drawing of Santa Claus riding his sleigh across the moon.

CHAPTER 38

Coda

'HAPPY CHRISTMAS!' said Bonny as she brought out from the kitchen an enormous turkey (made in a laboratory – one good thing about this future Christmas is that no animals were killed any more for people's Christmas dinners). She set it down on the table.

'HAPPY CHRISTMAS, MUM!' said Etta and Jonas. On the television, which was playing on a wall nearby, there were scenes from everywhere in the world of children opening presents and being happy. Somewhere, someone was playing 'It's the Most Wonderful Time of the Year'.

'Yes, Happy Christmas, Bonny!' said Gary.

Bonny smiled at him. Etta's dad hadn't spent Christmas with them since he and Etta's mum had separated. But this one felt different. So here he was.

'Happy Christmas!' said Monty, who was there too.

'Meow!' said Weech, who was sitting at Etta's feet. He was looking up at her, hoping for scraps, and wearing a very sparkly collar indeed.

'He looks amazing!' said Gary.

'Thanks so much for Weech's collar, Mum and Dad!' said Etta.

'Well . . .' said Bonny, 'I didn't actually buy it for you. It was in your stocking . . .'

'I know. But thanks anyway. I don't think Santa

would have been able to deliver it without both of your help!'

Bonny and Gary exchanged glances again. But this time with a smile.

'How was the mince pie? And the carrot? And the glass of sherry?' she asked.

'All eaten and drunk!' said Gary. And Etta noticed him glance over at the Christmas tree, where, earlier, he had hung the bauble

from Grandma Jo's box. The one he had made as a little boy. 'Well, what a Christmas it's been!'

'Amazing,' said Etta. 'Also amazing,' she continued, holding up her phone, 'is the number of children online talking about their presents, and posting about how strange and wrong it is that some people are saying Santa isn't real. People, apparently, including all these weird new accounts that have just been registered online . . .'

'Hmm. For "weird" should we read "Winterzone"?' said Bonny.

'I can't possibly comment,' said Etta. 'But those nasty ones are completely outnumbered by the nice ones saying things like: "Here's my present – so Santa's real all right!"'

'Santa!' said Jonas. And everyone smiled.

'For me,' said Monty, 'the *most* amazing moment was when Santa changed out of his overalls into his Santa suit.'

'Really? That was your most amazing moment?' said Bonny.

'Yes. Who knew he wore such big Y-fronts? With little Christmas trees on them too!'

'You are a funny fellow, Monty,' said Gary. 'Shall we pull a cracker, Etta?'

'Yes,' she said. 'What about this one?'

She produced from under the table a gold one. *The* gold one. The one that had been in her white shoebox.

Gary frowned. 'You sure?'

'Of course. It's time. Now that Christmas *is* Christmas. It's what Grandma Jo would've wanted!'

Gary's eyes moistened a little. 'OK . . .'

Etta held out an end for him. They pulled at it together and . . . BANG! It came apart. Not just in two bits, but seemingly everywhere – little bits of gold in a small cloud covering the whole table.

'OOH!' said Jonas.

'Wow!' said Etta.

'Is there a joke inside?' said Monty.

Etta looked down. 'No. A rubbish paper crown. Obviously. And . . . oh yes.' She opened up a little blue bit of tissue paper. 'Well, it's more a kind of . . . *saying* than a joke.' It was written in curly red letters. She read out:

'CHRISTMAS WAVES A
MAGIC WAND OVER THE WORLD,
AND BEHOLD — EVERYTHING IS
SOFTER AND MORE BEAUTIFUL.'

'Aaah,' said Bonny.

'How lovely,' said Gary.

'Well, it's not up there with "What goes oh oh oh? – Santa walking backwards,"' said Monty.

'Good one, Monty,' said Gary.

'Thanks. I'm off now.'

'You're going?' asked Etta.

'Yes! Sorry – it's been lovely, but I've got to go home . . .'

'Really?' said Bonny. 'But it's Christmas!'

'I know. I don't celebrate it. Come on, guys. Monty Cohen?' He smiled, jumped down from his chair, and put his coat on. 'Happy Chanukah!'